EVERYMAN,
I WILL GO WITH THEE,
AND BE THY GUIDE,
IN THY MOST NEED
TO GO BY THY SIDE

KATE CHOPIN

THE
AWAKENING
A SOLITARY SOUL

WITH AN INTRODUCTION
BY ELAINE SHOWALTER

EVERYMAN'S LIBRARY
Alfred A. Knopf   New York London Toronto

132

THIS IS A BORZOI BOOK
PUBLISHED BY ALFRED A. KNOPF

First included in Everyman's Library, 1992
Introduction first published in *New Essays on The Awakening*, 1988.
Reproduced by kind permission of Cambridge University Press and
Elaine Showalter.
Bibliography and Chronology Copyright © 1992
by Everyman's Library
Typography by Peter B. Willberg
Tenth printing (US)

www.randomhouse.com/everymans
www.everymanslibrary.co.uk

ISBN: 978-0-679-41721-7 (US)
978-1-85715-132-9 (UK)

A CIP catalogue reference for this book is available from the
British Library

Library of Congress Cataloging-in-Publication Data
Chopin, Kate, 1851–1904.
The awakening/Kate Chopin.
p.   cm.—(Everyman's library)
ISBN 978-0-679-41721-7
I. Title.
PS1294.C63A6   1992   92-52897
813'.4—dc20   CIP

Book design by Barbara de Wilde and Carol Devine Carson

Printed and bound in Germany by GGP Media GmbH, Pössneck

THE AWAKENING

INTRODUCTION

'Whatever we may do or attempt, despite the embrace and transports of love, the hunger of the lips, we are always alone. I have dragged you out into the night in the vain hope of a moment's escape from the horrible solitude which overpowers me. But what is the use! I speak and you answer me, and still each of us is alone; side by side but alone.' In 1895, these words, from a story by Guy de Maupassant called 'Solitude', which she had translated for a St Louis magazine, expressed an urbane and melancholy wisdom that Kate Chopin found compelling. To a woman who had survived the illusions that friendship, romance, marriage, or even motherhood would provide lifelong companionship and identity, and who had come to recognize the existential solitude of all human beings, Maupassant's declaration became a kind of credo. Indeed, *The Awakening*, which Chopin subtitled 'A Solitary Soul', may be read as an account of Edna Pontellier's evolution from romantic fantasies of fusion with another person to self-definition and self-reliance. At the beginning of the novel, in the midst of the bustling social world of Grand Isle, caught in her domestic roles of wife and mother, Edna pictures solitude as alien, masculine, and frightening, a naked man standing beside a 'desolate rock' by the sea in an attitude of 'hopeless resignation'. By the end, she has claimed a solitude that is defiantly feminine, returning to the nearly empty island off-season, to stand naked and 'absolutely alone' by the shore and to elude 'the soul's slavery' by plunging into the sea's embrace.

Yet Edna's triumphant embrace of solitude could not be the choice of Kate Chopin as an artist. A writer may work in solitude but literature depends on a tradition, on shared forms and representations of experience; and literary genres, like biological species, evolve because of significant innovations by individuals that survive through imitation and revision. Thus it can be a very serious blow to a developing genre when a revolutionary work is taken out of circulation Experimentation is retarded and repressed, and it may be several generations before the evolution of the literary genre catches up. The interruption of this evolutionary process is most destructive for the literature of a minority group, in which writers have to contend with cultural prejudices against their creative gifts. Yet radical departures from literary convention within a minority tradition are especially likely to be censured and suppressed by the dominant culture, because they violate social as well as aesthetic stereotypes and expectations.

The Awakening was just such a revolutionary book. Generally recognized today as the first aesthetically successful novel to have been written by an American woman, it marked a significant epoch in the evolution of an American female literary tradition. As an American woman novelist of the 1890s, Kate Chopin had inherited a rich and compelx tradition, composed not only of her American female precursors but also of American transcendentalism, European realism, and *fin-de-siècle* feminism and aestheticism. In this context *The Awakening* broke new ground. Chopin went boldly beyond the work of her precursors in writing about women's longing for sexual and personal emancipation. Yet the novel represents a literary beginning as abruptly cut off as its heroine's awakening consciousness. Edna Pontellier's explicit violations of the modes and codes of nineteenth-century American women's behavior shocked contemporary critics, who described *The Awakening* as 'morbid', 'essentially vulgar', and 'gilded dirt'. Banned in Kate Chopin's own city of St Louis and censured in the national press, *The Awakening* thus became a solitary book, one that dropped out of sight and remained unsung by literary historians and unread by several generations of American women writers.

In many respects, *The Awakening* seems to comment on its own history as a novel, to predict its own critical fate. The parallels between the experiences of Edna Pontellier, as she breaks away from the conventional feminine roles of wife and mother, and Kate Chopin, as she breaks away from conventions of literary domesticity, suggest that Edna's story may also be read as a parable of Chopin's literary awakening. Both the author and the heroine seem to be oscillating between two worlds, caught between contradictory definitions of femininity and creativity, and seeking either to synthesize them or to go beyond them to an emancipated womanhood and an emancipated fiction. Edna Pontellier's 'unfocused yearning' for an autonomous life is akin to Kate Chopin's yearning to write works that go beyond female plots and feminine endings.

In the early stages of her career, Chopin had tried to follow the literary advice and example of others and had learned that such dutiful efforts led only to imaginative stagnation. By the late 1890s, when she wrote *The Awakening*, she had come to believe that the true artist was one who defied tradition, who rejected both the 'convenances' of respectable morality and the conventions and formulas of literary success. What impressed her most about Maupassant was that he had 'escaped from tradition and authority ... had entered into himself and looked out upon life through this own being and with his own eyes'. This is very close to what happens to Edna Pontellier as she frees herself from social obligations and received opinions and begins 'to look with her own eyes; to see and to apprehend the deeper undercurrents of life'. Much as she admired Maupassant, and much as she learned from translating his work, Chopin felt no desire to imitate him. Her sense of the need for independence and individuality in writing is dramatically expressed in *The Awakening* by Mademoiselle Reisz, who tells Edna that the artist must possess 'the courageous soul that dares and defies' and must have strong wings to soar 'above the level plain of tradition and prejudice'.

Nonetheless, in order to understand *The Awakening* fully, we need to read it in the context of literary tradition. Even in its defiant solitude, *The Awakening* speaks for a transitional phase in American women's writing, and Chopin herself would never have written the books she did without a tradition to admire and oppose. When she wrote *The Awakening* in 1899, she could look back to at least two generations of female literary precursors. The antebellum novelists, led by Harriet Beecher Stowe, Susan Warner, and E.D.E.N. Southworth, were the first members of these generations. Born in the early decades of the nineteenth century, they began to publish stories and novels in the 1850s and 1860s that reflected the dominant expressive and symbolic models of an American woman's culture.

The historian Carroll Smith-Rosenberg has called this culture the 'female world of love and ritual', and it was primarily defined by the veneration of motherhood, by intense mother–daughter bonds, and by intimate female friendships. Although premarital relationships between the sexes were subject to severe restrictions, romantic friendships between women were admired and encouraged. The nineteenth-century ideal of female 'passionlessness' – the belief that women did not have the same sexual desires as men – had advantages as well as disadvantages for women. It reinforced the notion that women were the purer and more spiritual sex, and thus were morally superior to men. Furthermore, as the historian Nancy F. Cott has argued, 'acceptance of the idea of passionlessness created sexual solidarity among women; it allowed women to consider their love relationships with one another of higher character than heterosexual relationships because they excluded (male) carnal passion.' 'I do not believe that men can ever feel so pure an enthusiasm for women as we can feel for one another,' wrote the novelist Catherine Sedgwick. 'Ours is nearest to the love of angels.' The homosocial world of women's culture in fact allowed much leeway for physical intimacy and touch; 'girls routinely slept together, kissed and hugged one another.' But these caresses were not interpreted as erotic expressions.

The mid-nineteenth-century code of values growing out of women's culture, which Mary Ryan calls 'the empire of the mother', was also sustained by sermons, child-rearing manuals, and sentimental fiction. Women writers advocated motherly influence – 'gentle nurture', 'sweet control', and 'educating power' – as an effective solution to such social problems as alcoholism, crime, slavery, and war. As Harriet Beecher Stowe proclaimed, 'The Woman Question' of the day is: Shall MOTHERHOOD ever be felt in the public administration of the affairs of state?'

As writers, however, the sentimentalists looked to motherhood for their metaphors and justifications of literary creativity. 'Creating a story is like bearing a child,' wrote Stowe, 'and it leaves me in as weak and helpless a state as when my baby was born.' Pre-Civil War women's fiction, variously described as 'literary domesticity' or the 'sentimental novel', celebrates matriarchal institutions and idealizes the period of blissful bonding between mother and child. It is permeated by the artifacts, spaces, and images of nineteenth-century American domestic culture: the kitchen, with its worn rocking chair; the Edenic mother's garden, with its fragrant female flowers and energetic male bees; the caged songbird, which represents the creative woman in her domestic sphere. Women's narratives were formally composed of brief sketches joined together like the pieces of a patchwork quilt; they frequently alluded to specific quilt patterns and followed quilt design conventions of repetition, variation, and contrast. Finally, their most intense representation of female sexual pleasure was not in terms of heterosexual romance, but rather the holding or suckling of a baby; for, as Mary Ryan points out, 'nursing an infant was one of the most hallowed and inviolate episodes in a woman's life ... Breast-feeding was sanctioned as "one of the most important duties of female life", "one of peculiar, inexpressible felicity", and "the sole occupation and pleasure" of a new mother.'

The cumulative effect of all these covert appeals to female solidarity in books written by, for, and about women could be a subversive critique of patriarchal power. Yet aesthetically the fiction of this generation was severely restricted. The sentimentalists did not identify with the figure of the 'artist', the 'genius', or the 'poet' promulgated by patriarchal culture. As Nina Baym explains, 'they conceptualized authorship as a profession rather than a calling ... Women authors tended not to think of themselves as artists or justify themselves in the language of art until the 1870s and after.' In the writing of the sentimentalists, 'the dimensions of formal self-consciousness, attachment to or quarrel with a grand tradition, aesthetic seriousness, are all missing. Often the women deliberately and even proudly disavowed membership in an artistic fraternity.' Insofar as art implied a male club or circle of brothers, women felt excluded from it. Instead they claimed affiliation with a literary sorority, a society of sisters whose motives were moral rather than aesthetic, whose ambitions were to teach and to influence rather than to create. Although their books sold by the millions, they were not taken seriously by male critics.

The next generation of American women writers, however, found themselves in a different cultural situation. After the Civil War, the homosocial world of women's culture began to dissolve as women demanded entrance to higher education, the professions, and the political world. The female local colorists who began to publish stories about American regional life in the 1870s and 1880s were also attracted to the male worlds of art and prestige opening up to women, and they began to assert themselves as daughters of literary fathers as well as literary mothers. Claiming both male and female aesthetic models, they felt free to present themselves as artists and to write confidently about the art of fiction in such essays as Elizabeth Stuart Phelps' 'Art for Truth's Sake'. Among the differences the local colorists saw between themselves and their predecessors was the question of 'selfishness', the ability to put literary ambitions before domestic duties. Although she had been strongly influenced in her work by Harriet Beecher Stowe's *Pearl of Orr's Island*, Sarah Orne Jewett came to believe that Stowe's work was 'incomplete' because she was unable to 'bring herself to that cold selfishness of the moment for one's work's sake'.

Writers of this generation chose to put their work first. The 1870s and 1880s were what Susan B. Anthony called 'an epoch of single women', and many unmarried women writers of this generation lived alone; others were involved in 'Boston marriages', or long-term relationships with another woman. But despite their individual lifestyles, many speculated in their writing on the conflicts between maternity and artistic creativity. Motherhood no longer seemed to be the motivating force of writing, but rather its opposite. Thus artistic fulfillment required the sacrifice of maternal drives, and maternal fulfillment meant giving up artistic ambitions.

The conflicts between love and work that Edna Pontellier faces in *The Awakening* were anticipated in such earlier novels as Louisa May Alcott's unfinished *Diana and Persis* (1879) and Elizabeth Stuart Phelps' *The Story of Avis* (1879). A gifted painter who has studied in Florence and Paris, Avis does not intend to marry. As she tells her suitor, 'My ideals of art are those with which marriage is perfectly incompatible. Success – for a woman – means absolute surrender, in whatever direction. Whether she paints a picture, or loves a man, there is no division of labor possible in her economy. To the attainment of any end worth living for, a symmetrical sacrifice of her nature is compulsory upon her.' But love persuades her to change her mind, and the novel records the inexorable destruction of her artistic genius as domestic responsibilities, maternal cares, and her husband's failures use up her energy. By the end of the novel, Avis has become resigned to the idea that her life is a sacrifice for the next generation of women. Thinking back to her mother, a talented actress who gave up her profession to marry and died young, and looking at her daughter, Wait, Avis takes heart in the hope that it may take three generations to create the woman who can unite 'her supreme capacity of love' with the 'sacred individuality of her life'. As women's culture declined after the Civil War, moreover, the local colorists mourned its demise by investing its traditional images with mythic significance. In their stories, the mother's garden has become a paradisal sanctuary; the caged bird a wild white heron, or heroine of nature; the house an emblem of the female body, with the kitchen as its womb; and the artifacts of domesticity virtually totemic objects. In Jewett's *Country of the Pointed Firs*, for example, the braided rag rug has become a kind of prayer mat of concentric circles from which the matriarchal priestess, Mrs Todd, delivers her sybilline pronouncements. The woman artist in this fiction expresses her conflicting needs most fully in her quasi-religious dedication to these artifacts of a bygone age.

The New Women writers of the 1890s no longer grieved for the female bonds and sanctuaries of the past. Products of both Darwinian skepticism and aesthetic sophistication, they had an ambivalent or even hostile relationship to women's culture, which they often saw as boring and restrictive. Their attitudes toward female sexuality were also revolutionary. A few radical feminists had always maintained that women's sexual apathy was not an innately feminine attribute but rather the result of prudery and repression; some women's rights activists too had privately confessed that, as Elizabeth Cady Stanton wrote in her diary in 1883, 'a healthy woman has as much passion as a man'. Not all New Women advocated female sexual emancipation; the most zealous advocates of free love were male novelists such as Grant Allen, whose bestseller, *The Woman Who Did* (1895), became a byword of the decade. But the heroine of New Woman fiction, as Linda Dowling has explained, 'expressed her quarrel with Victorian culture chiefly through sexual means – by heightening sexual consciousness, candor, and expression'. No wonder, then, that reviewers saw *The Awakening* as part of the 'overworked field of sex fiction' or noted that since 'San Francisco and Paris, and London, and New York had furnished Women Who Did, why not New Orleans?'

In the form as well as the content of their work, New Women writers demanded freedom and innovation. They modified the realistic three-decker novels about courtship and marriage that had formed the bulk of mid-century 'woman's fiction' to make room for interludes of fantasy and parable, especially episodes 'in which a woman will dream of an entirely different world or will cross-dress, experimenting with the freedom available to boys and men'. Instead of the crisply plotted short stories that had been the primary genre of the local colorists, writers such as Olive Schreiner, Ella D'Arcy, Sarah Grand, and 'George Egerton' (Mary Chavelita Dunne) experimented with new fictional forms that they called 'keynotes', 'allegories', 'fantasies', 'monochromes', or 'dreams'. As Egerton explained, these impressionistic narratives were efforts to explore a hitherto unrecorded female consciousness: 'I realized that in literature everything had been done better by man than woman could hope to emulate. There was only one small plot left for herself to tell: the *terra incognita* of herself, as she knew herself to be, not as man liked to imagine her – in a word to give herself away, as man had given himself away in his writings.'

Kate Chopin's literary evolution took her progressively through the three phases of nineteenth-century American women's culture and women's writing. Born in 1850, she grew up with the great bestsellers of the American and English sentimentalists. As a girl, she had wept over the works of Warner and Stowe and had copied pious passages from the English novelist Dinah Mulock Craik's *The Woman's Kingdom* into her diary. Throughout her adolescence, Chopin had also shared an intimate friendship with Kitty Garasché, a classmate at the Academy of the Sacred Heart. Together, Chopin recalled, the girls had read fiction and poetry, gone on excursions, and 'exchanged our heart secrets'. Their friendship ended in 1870 when Kate Chopin married and Kitty Garasché entered a convent. Yet when Oscar Chopin died in 1883, his young widow went to visit her old friend and was shocked by her blind isolation from the world. When Chopin began to write, she took as her models such local colorists as Sarah Orne Jewett and Mary Wilkins Freeman, who had not only mastered technique and constuction but had also devoted themselves to telling the stories of female loneliness, isolation, and frustration.

Sandra Gilbert has suggested that local color was a narrative strategy that Chopin employed to solve a specific problem: how to deal with extreme psychological states without the excesses of sentimental narrative and without critical recrimination. At first, Gilbert suggests, 'local color' writing 'offered both a mode and a manner that could mediate between the literary structures she had inherited and those she had begun'. Like the anthropologist, the local colorist could observe vagaries of culture and character with 'almost scientific detachment'. Furthermore, 'by reporting odd events and customs that were part of a region's "local color" she could tell what would ordinarily be rather shocking or even melodramatic tales in an unmelodramatic way, and without fear of ... moral outrage'.

But before long, Chopin looked beyond the oddities of the local colorists to more ambitous models. Her literary tastes were anything but parochial. She read widely in a variety of genres – Darwin, Spencer, and Huxley, as well as Aristophanes, Flaubert, Whitman, Swinburne, and Ibsen. In particular, she associated her own literary and psychological awakening with Maupassant. 'Here was life, not fiction,' she wrote of his influence on her; 'for where were the plots, the old fashioned mechanism and stage trapping that in a vague, unthinking way I had fancied were essential to the art of story making.' In a review of a book by the local colorist Hamlin Garland, Chopin expressed her dissatisfaction with the restricted subjects of regional writing: 'Social problems, social environments, local color, and the rest of it' could not 'insure the survival of a writer who employs them'. She resented being compared to George Washington Cable or Grace King. Furthermore, she did not share the femal local colorists' obsession with the past, their desperate nostalgia for a bygone idealized age. 'How curiously the past effaces itself for me!' she wrote in her diary in 1894. 'I cannot live through yesterday or tomorrow.' Unlike Jewett, Freeman, King, or Woolson, she did not favor the old woman as narrator.

Despite her identification with the New Women, however, Chopin was not an activist. She never joined the women's suffrage movement or belonged to a female literary community. Indeed, her celebrated St Louis literary salon attracted mostly male journalists, editors, and writers. Chopin resigned after only two years from a St Louis women's literary and charitable society. When her children identified her close friends to be interviewed by her first biographer, Daniel Rankin, there were no women on the list.

Thus Chopin certainly did not wish to write a didactic feminist novel. In reviews published in the 1890s, she indicated her impatience with novelists such as Zola and Hardy, who tried to instruct their readers. She distrusted the rhetoric of such feminist bestsellers as Sarah Grand's *The Heavenly Twins* (1893). The eleventh commandment, she noted, is 'Thou shalt not preach'. Instead she would try to record, in her own way and in her own voice, the *terra incognita* of a woman's 'inward life' in all its 'vague, tangled, chaotic' tumult.

Much of the shock effect of *The Awakening* to the readers of 1899 came from Chopin's rejection of the conventions of women's writing. Despite her name, which echoes two famous heroines of the domestic novel (Edna Earl in Augusta Evans' *St. Elmo* and Edna Kenderdine in Dinah Craik's *The Woman's*

Kingdom), Edna Pontellier appears to reject the domestic empire of the mother and the sororal world of women's culture. Seemingly beyond the bonds of womanhood, she has neither mother nor daughter, and even refuses to go to her sister's wedding.

Moreover, whereas the sentimental heroine nurtures others, and the abstemious local color heroine subsists upon meager vegetarian diets, Kate Chopin's heroine is a robust woman who does not deny her appetites. Freeman's New England nun picks at her dainty lunch of lettuce leaves and currants, but Edna Pontellier eats hearty meals of paté, pompano, steak, and broiled chicken; bites off chunks of crusty bread; snacks on beer and Gruyère cheese; and sips brandy, wine, and champagne.

Formally, too, the novel has moved away from conventional techniques of realism to an impressionistic rhythm of epiphany and mood. Chopin abandoned the chapter titles she had used in her first novel, *At Fault* (1890), for thirty-nine numbered chapters of uneven length, ranging from the single paragraph of Chapter 28 to the sustained narrative of the dinner party in Chapter 30. The chapters are unified less by their style than by their focus on Edna's consciousness, and by the repetition of key motifs and images: music, the sea, shadows, swimming, eating, sleeping, gambling, the lovers, birth. Chapters of lyricism and fantasy, such as Edna's voyage to the Chênière Caminada, alternate with realistic, even satirical, scenes of Edna's marriage.

Most important, where previous works ignored sexuality or spiritualized it through maternity, *The Awakening* is insistently sexual, explicitly involved with the body and with self-awareness through physical awareness. Although Edna's actual seduction by Arobin takes place in the narrative neverland between Chapters 31 and 32, Chopin brilliantly evokes sexuality through images and details. In keeping with the novel's emphasis on the self, several scenes suggest Edna's initial auto-eroticism. Edna's midnight swim, which awakens the 'first-felt throbbings of desire', takes place in an atmosphere of erotic fragrance, 'strange, rare odors ... a tangle of the sea-smell and of weeds and damp new-plowed earth, mingled with the heavy perfume of a field of white blossoms'. A similarly voluptuous scene is her nap at Chênière Caminada, when she examines her flesh as she lies in a 'strange, quaint bed with its sweet country odor of laurel'.

Edna reminds Dr Mandelet of 'some beautiful, sleek animal waking up in the sun', and we recall that among her fantasies in listening to music is the image of a lady stroking a cat. The image both conveys Edna's sensuality and hints at the self-contained, almost masturbatory, quality of her sexuality. Her rendez-vous with Robert takes place in a sunny garden where both stroke a drowsy cat's silky fur, and Arobin first seduces her by smoothing her hair with his 'soft, magnetic hand'.

Yet despite these departures from tradition, there are other respects in which the novel seems very much of its time. As its title suggests, *The Awakening* is a novel about a process rather than a program, about a passage rather than a destination. Like Edith Wharton's *The House of Mirth* (1905), it is a transitional female fiction of the *fin-de-siècle*, a narrative of and about the passage from the homosocial women's culture and literature of the nineteenth century to the heterosexual fiction of modernism. Chopin might have taken the plot from a notebook entry Henry James made in 1892 about 'the growing divorce between the American woman (with her comparative leisure, culture, grace, social instincts, artistic ambition) and the male American immersed in the ferocity of business, with no time for any but the most sordid interests, purely commercial, professional, democratic and political. This divorce is rapidly becoming a gulf.' The Gulf where the opening chapters of *The Awakening* are set certainly suggests the 'growing divorce' between Edna's interests and desires and Léonce's obsessions with the stock market, property, and his brokerage business.

Yet in turning away from her marriage, Edna initially looks back to women's culture rather than forward to another man. As Sandra Gilbert has pointed out, Grand Isle is an oasis of women's culture, or a 'female colony': 'Madame Lebrun's pension on Grand Isle is very much a woman's land not only because it is owned and run by a single woman and dominated by 'mother-women' but also because (as in so many summer colonies today) its principal inhabitants are actually women and children whose husbands and fathers visit only at week-ends ... [and it is situated], like so many places that are significant for women, outside patriarchal culture, beyond the limits and limitations of the city where men make history, on a shore that marks the margin where nature intersects with culture.'

Edna's awakening, moreover, begins not with a man, but with Adèle Ratignolle, the empress of the 'mother-women' of Grand Isle. A 'self-contained' woman, Edna has never had any close relationships with members of her own sex. Thus it is Adèle who belatedly initiates Edna into the world of female love and ritual on the first step of her sensual voyage of self-discovery. Edna's first attraction to Adèle is physical: 'the excessive physical charm of the Creole had first attracted her, for Edna had a sensuous susceptibility to beauty'. At the beach, in the hot sun, she responds to Adèle's caresses, the first she has ever known from another woman, as Adèle clasps her hand 'firmly and warmly' and strokes it fondly. The touch provokes Edna to an unaccustomed candor; leaning her head on Adèle's shoulder and confiding some of her secrets, she begins to feel 'intoxicated'. The bond between them goes beyond sympathy, as Chopin notes, to 'what we might well call love'.

In some respects, the motherless Edna also seeks a mother surrogate in Adèle and looks to her for nurturance. Adèle provides maternal encouragement for Edna's painting and tells her that her 'talent is immense'. Characteristically, Adèle has rationalized her own 'art' as a maternal project: 'she was keeping up her music on account of the children ... a means of brightening the home and making it attractive.' Edna's responses to Adèle's music have been similarly tame and sentimental. Her revealing fantasies as she listens to Adèle play her easy pieces suggest the restriction and decorum of the female world: 'a dainty young woman ... taking mincing dancing steps, as she came down a long avenue between tall hedges'; 'children at play'. Women's art, as Adèle presents it, is social, pleasant, and undemanding. It does not conflict with her duties as a wife and mother, and can even be seen to enhance them. Edna understands this well; as she retorts when her husband recommends Adèle as a model of an artist, 'She isn't a musician and I'm not a painter!'

Yet the relationship with the conventional Adèle educates the immature Edna to respond for the first time both to a different kind of sexuality and to the unconventional and difficult art of Mademoiselle Reisz. In responding to Adèle's interest, Edna begins to think about her own past and to analyse her own personality. In textual terms, it is through this relationship that she becomes 'Edna' in the narrative rather than 'Mrs Pontellier'.

We see the next stage of Edna's awakening in her relationship with Mademoiselle Reisz, who initiates her into the world of art. Significantly, this passage also takes place through a female rather than a male mentor, and, as with Adèle, there is something more intense than friendship between the two women. Whereas Adèle's fondness for Edna, however, is depicted as maternal and womanly, Mademoiselle Reisz's attraction to Edna suggests something more perverse. The pianist is obsessed with Edna's beauty, raves over her figure in a bathing suit, greets her as 'ma belle' and 'ma reine', holds her hand, and describes herself as 'a foolish old woman whom you have captivated'. If Adèle is a surrogate for Edna's dead mother and the intimate friend she never had as a girl, Mademoiselle Reisz, whose music reduces Edna to passionate sobs, seems to be a surrogate lover. And whereas Adèle is a 'faultless madonna' who speaks for the values and laws of the Creole community, Mademoiselle Reisz is a renegade, self-assertive and outspoken. She has no patience with petty social rules and violates the most basic expectations of femininity. To a rake like Arobin, she is so unattractive, unpleasant, and unwomanly as to seem 'partially demented'. Even Edna occasionally perceives Mademoiselle Reisz's awkwardness as a kind of deformity; she is sometimes offended by the old woman's candor and is not sure whether she likes her.

Yet despite her eccentricities, Mademoiselle Reisz seems 'to reach Edna's spirit and set it free'. Her voice in the novel seems to speak for the author's view of art and for the artist. It is surely no accident, for example, that it is Chopin's music that

Mademoiselle Reisz performs. At the *pension* on Grand Isle, the pianist first plays a Chopin prelude, to which Edna responds with surprising turbulence: 'the very passions themselves were aroused within her soul, swaying it, lashing it, as the waves daily beat upon her splendid body. She trembled, she was choking, and the tears blinded her.' 'Chopin' becomes the code word for a world of repressed passion between Edna and Robert that Mademoiselle Reisz controls. Later the pianist plays a Chopin impromptu for Edna that Robert has admired; this time the music is 'strange and fantastic – turbulent, plaintive and soft with entreaty'. These references to 'Chopin' in the text are on one level allusions to an intimate, romantic, and poignant musical *oeuvre* that reinforces the novel's sensual atmosphere. But on another level, they function as what Nancy K. Miller has called the 'internal female signature' in women's writing, here a literary punning signature that alludes to Kate Chopin's ambitions as an artist and to the emotions she wished her book to arouse in its readers.

Chopin's career represented one important aesthetic model for his literary namesake. As a girl, Kate Chopin had been a talented musician, and her first published story, 'Wiser Than a God', was about a woman concert pianist who refused to marry. Moreover, Chopin's music influences the language and form of *The Awakening*. The structure of the impromptu, in which there is an opening presentation of a theme, a contrasting middle section, and a modified return to the melodic and rhythmic materials of the opening section, parallels the narrative form of *The Awakening*. The composer's techniques of unifying his work through the repetition of musical phrases, his experiments with harmony and dissonance, his use of folk motifs, his effects of frustration and delayed resolution can also be compared to Kate Chopin's repetition of sentences, her juxtaposition of realism and impressionism, her incorporation of local color elements, and her rejection of conventional closure.

Madame Ratignolle and Mademoiselle Reisz not only represent important alternative roles and influences for Edna in the world of the novel, but as the proto-heroines of sentimental and local color fiction, they also suggest different plots and conclusions. Adèle's story suggests that Edna will give up her rebellion, return to her marriage, have another baby, and by degrees learn to appreciate, love, and even desire her husband. Such was the plot of many late-nineteenth-century sentimental novels about erring young women married to older men. Mademoiselle Reisz's story suggests that Edna will lose her beauty, her youth, her husband, and children – everything, in short, but her art and her pride – and become a kind of New Orleans nun.

Chopin wished to reject both of these endings and to escape from the literary traditions they represented; but her own literary solitude, her resistance to allying herself with a specific ideological or aesthetic position, made it impossible for her to work out something different and new. Edna remains very much entangled in her own emotions and moods, rather than moving beyond them to real self-understanding and to an awareness of her relationship to her society. She alternates between two moods of 'intoxication' and 'languor', expansive states of activity, optimism, and power and passive states of contemplation, despondency, and sexual thralldom. Edna feels intoxicated when she is assertive and in control. She first experiences such exultant feelings when she confides her story to Adèle Ratignolle and again when she learns how to swim: 'intoxicated with her newly conquered power', she swims out too far. She is excited when she gambles successfully for high stakes at the race track, and finally she feels 'an intoxication of expectancy' about awakening Robert with a seductive kiss and playing the dominant role with him. But these emotional peaks are countered by equally intense moods of depression, reverie, or stupor. At the worst, these are states of 'indescribable oppression', 'vague anguish', or 'hopeless ennui'. At best, they are moments of passive sensuality in which Edna feels drugged; Arobin's lips and hands, for example, act 'like a narcotic upon her'.

Edna welcomes both kinds of feelings because they are intense, and thus preserve her from the tedium of ordinary existence. They are in fact adolescent emotions, suitable to a heroine who is belatedly awakening; but Edna does not go beyond them to an adulthood that offers new experiences or responsibilities. In her relationships with men, she both longs for complete and romantic fusion with a fantasy lover and is unprepared to share her life with another person.

Chopin's account of the Pontellier marriage, for example, shows Edna's tacit collusion in a sexual bargain that allows her to keep to herself. Although she thinks of her marriage to a paternalistic man twelve years her senior as 'purely an accident', the text makes it clear that Edna has married Léonce primarily to secure a fatherly protector who will not make too many domestic, emotional, or sexual demands on her. She is 'fond of her husband', with 'no trace of passion or excessive or fictitious warmth'. They do not have an interest in each other's activities or thoughts, and have agreed to a complete separation of their social spheres; Léonce is fully absorbed by the business, social, and sexual activities of the male sphere, the city, Carondelet Street, Klein's Hotel at Grand Isle, where he gambles, and especially the New Orleans world of the clubs and the red-light district. Even Adèle Ratignolle warns Edna of the risks of Mr Pontellier's club life and of the 'diversion' he finds there. 'Its a pity Mr Pontellier doesn't stay home more in the evenings', she tells Edna. 'I think you would be more – well, if you don't mind my saying it – more united, if he did.' 'Oh! dear no!' Edna responds, 'with a blank look in her eyes. "What should I do if he stayed home? We wouldn't have anything to say to each other"'. Edna gets this blank look in her eyes – eyes that are originally described as 'quick and bright' – whenever she is confronted with something she does not want to see. When she joins the Ratignolles at home together, Edna does not envy them, although, as the author remarks, 'if ever the fusion of two human beings into one has been accomplished on this sphere it was surely in their union'. Instead, she is moved by pity for Adèle's 'colorless existence which never uplifted its possessor beyond the region of blind contentment'.

Nonetheless, Edna does not easily relinquish her fantasy of rhapsodic oneness with a perfect lover. She imagines that such a union will bring permanent ecstasy; it will lead, not simply to 'domestic harmony' like that of the Ratignolles, but to 'life's delirium'. In her story of the woman who paddles away with her lover in a pirogue and is never heard of again, Edna elaborates on her vision as she describes the lovers, 'close together, rapt in oblivious forgetfulness, drifting into the unknown'. Although her affair with Arobin shocks her into an awareness of her own sexual passions, it leaves her illusions about love intact. Desire, she understands, can exist independently of love. But love retains its magical aura; indeed, her sexual awakening with Arobin generates an even 'fiercer, more overpowering love' for Robert. And when Robert comes back, Edna has persuaded herself that the force of their love will overwhelm all obstacles: 'We shall be everything to each other. Nothing else in the world is of any consequence.' Her intention seems to be that they will go off together into the unknown, like the lovers in her story. But Robert cannot accept such a role, and when he leaves her, Edna finally realizes 'that the day would come when he, too, and the thought of him, would melt out of her existence, leaving her alone'.

The other side of Edna's terror of solitude, however, is the bondage of class as well as gender that keeps her in a prison of the self. She goes blank too whenever she might be expected to notice the double standard of ladylike privilege and oppression of women in southern society. Floating along in her 'mazes of inward contemplation', Edna barely notices the silent quadroon nurse who takes care of her children, the little black girl who works the treadles of Madame Lebrun's sewing machine, the laundress who keeps her in frilly white, or the maid who picks up her broken glass. She never makes connections between her lot and theirs.

The scene in which Edna witnesses Adèle in childbirth is the first time in the novel that she identifies with another woman's pain, and draws some halting conclusions about the female and the human condition, rather than simply about her own ennui. Edna's births have taken place in unconsciousness; when she goes to Adèle's childbed, 'her own like experiences seemed far away, unreal, and only half remembered. She recalled faintly an ecstasy of pain, the heavy odor of chloroform, a stupor which had deadened sensation.' The stupor that deadens sensation is an apt metaphor for the real and

imaginary narcotics supplied by fantasy, money, and patri-
archy, which have protected Edna from pain for most of her
life, but which have also kept her from becoming an adult.

But in thinking of nature's trap for women, Edna never
moves from her own questioning to the larger social statement
that is feminism. Her ineffectuality is partly a product of her
time; as a heroine in transition between the homosocial and
the heterosexual worlds, Edna has lost some of the sense of
connectedness to other women that might help her plan her
future. Though she has sojourned in the 'female colony' of
Grand Isle, it is far from being a feminist utopia, a real
community of women, in terms of sisterhood. The novel
suggests, in fact, something of the historical loss for women of
transferring the sense of self to relationships with men.

Edna's solitude is one of the reasons that her emancipation
does not take her very far. Despite her efforts to escape the
rituals of femininity, Edna seems fated to reenact them, even
though, as Chopin recounts these scenes, she satirizes and
revises their conventions. Ironically, considering her determination to discard the trappings of her role as a society matron
– her wedding ring, her 'reception day', her 'charming home'
– the high point of Edna's awakening is the dinner party she
gives for her twenty-ninth birthday. Edna's birthday party
begins like a kind of drawing-room comedy. We are told the
guest list, the seating plan, the menu, and the table setting;
some of the guests are boring, and some do not like each other;
Madame Ratignolle does not show up at the last minute, and
Mademoiselle Reisz makes disagreeable remarks in French.

Yet as it proceeds to its bacchanalian climax, the dinner
party also has a symbolic intensity and resonance that makes
it, as Sandra Gilbert argues, Edna's 'most authentic act of self-
definition'. Not only is the twenty-ninth birthday a feminine
threshold, the passage from youth to middle age, but Edna is
literally on the threshold of a new life in her little house. The
dinner, as Arobin remarks, is a *coup d'état*, an overthrow of her
marriage, all the more an act of aggression because Léonce
will pay the bills. Moreover, she has created an atmosphere of
splendor and luxury that seems to exceed the requirements of
the occasion. The table is set with gold satin, Sevres china,

crystal, silver, and gold; there is 'champagne to swim in', and Edna is magnificently dressed in a satin and lace gown, with a cluster of diamonds (a gift from Léonce) in her hair. Presiding at the head of the table, she seems powerful and autonomous: 'There was something in her attitude which suggested the regal woman, the one who rules, who looks on, who stands alone.' Edna's moment of mastery thus takes place in the context of a familiar ceremony of women's culture. Indeed, dinner parties are virtual set pieces of feminist aesthetics, suggesting that the hostess is a kind of artist in her own sphere, someone whose creativity is channelled into the production of social and domestic harmony. Like Virginia Woolf's Mrs Ramsay in *To the Lighthouse*, Edna exhausts herself in creating a sense of fellowship at her table, although in the midst of her guests she still experiences an 'acute longing' for 'the unattainable'.

But there is a gap between the intensity of Edna's desire, a desire that by now has gone beyond sexual fulfillment to take in a much vaster range of metaphysical longings, and the means that she has to express herself. Edna may look like a queen, but she is still a housewife. The political and aesthetic weapons she has in her *coup d'état* are only forks and knives, glasses and dresses.

Can Edna, and Kate Chopin, then, escape from confining traditions only in death? Some critics have seen Edna's much-debated suicide as a heroic embrace of independence and a symbolic resurrection into myth, a feminist counterpart of Melville's Bulkington: 'Take heart, take heart, O Edna, up from the spray of thy ocean-perishing, up, straight up, leaps thy apotheosis!' But the ending seems to return Edna to the nineteenth-century female literary tradition, even though Chopin redefines it for her own purpose. Readers of the 1890s were well accustomed to drowning as the fictional punishment for female transgression against morality, and most contemporary critics of *The Awakening* thus automatically interpreted Edna's suicide as the wages of sin.

Drowning itelf brings to mind metaphorical analogies between femininity and liquidity. As the female body is prone to wetness, blood, milk, tears, and amniotic fluid, so in drowning the woman is immersed in the feminine organic element. Drowning thus becomes the traditionally feminine literary death. And Edna's last thoughts further recycle significant images of the feminine from her past. As exhaustion overpowers her, 'Edna heard her father's voice and her sister Margaret's. She heard the barking of an old dog that was chained to the sycamore tree. The spurs of the cavalry officer clanged as he walked across the porch. There was the hum of bees, and the musky odor of pinks filled the air.' Edna's memories are those of awakening from the freedom of childhood to the limitations conferred by female sexuality.

The image of the bees and the flowers not only recalls early descriptions of Edna's sexuality as a 'sensitive blossom', but also places *The Awakening* firmly within the traditions of American women's writing, where it is a standard trope for the unequal sexual relations between women and men. Margaret Fuller, for example, writes in her journal: 'Woman is the flower, man the bee. She sighs out of melodious fragrance, and invites the winged laborer. He drains her cup, and carries off the honey. She dies on the stalk; he returns to the hive, well fed, and praised as an active member of the community.' In post-Civil War fiction, the image is a reminder of an elemental power that women's culture must confront. *The Awakening* seems particularly to echo the last lines of Mary Wilkins Freeman's 'A New England Nun', in which the heroine, having broken her long-standing engagement, is free to continue her solitary life, and closes her door on 'the sounds of the busy harvest of men and birds and bees; there were halloos, metallic clatterings, sweet calls, long hummings'. These are the images of a nature that, Edna has learned, decoys women into slavery; yet even in drowning, she cannot escape from their seductiveness, for to ignore their claim is also to cut oneself off from culture, from the 'humming' life of creation and achievement.

We can re-create the literary tradition in which Kate Chopin wrote *The Awakening*, but of course, we can never know how the tradition might have changed if her novel had not had to wait half a century to find its audience. Few of Chopin's literary contemporaries came into contact with the book. Chopin's biographer, Per Seyersted, notes that her work 'was apparently unknown to Dreiser, even though he began writing *Sister Carrie* just when *The Awakening* was being loudly condemned. Also Ellen Glasgow, who was at this time beginning to describe unsatisfactory marriages, seems to have been unaware of the author's existence. Indeed, we can safely say that though she was so much of an innovator in American literature, she was virtually unknown by those who were now to shape it and that she had no influence on them'. Ironically, even Willa Cather, the one woman writer of the *fin-de-siècle* who reviewed *The Awakening*, not only failed to recognize its importance but also dismissed its theme as 'trite'. It would be decades before another American woman novelist combined Kate Chopin's artistic maturity with her sophisticated outlook on sexuality, and overcame both the sentimental codes of feminine 'artlessness' and the sexual codes of feminine 'passionlessness'.

In terms of Chopin's own literary development, there were signs that *The Awakening* would have been a pivotal work. While it was in press, she wrote one of her finest and most daring short stories, 'The Storm', which surpasses even *The Awakening* in terms of its expressive freedom. Chopin was also being drawn back to a rethinking of women's culture. Her last poem, written in 1900, was addressed to Kitty Garesché and spoke of the permanence of emotional bonds between women:

To the Friend of My Youth

It is not all of life
To cling together while the years glide past.
It is not all of love
To walk with clasped hands from the first to last.
That mystic garland which the spring did twine
Of scented lilac and the new-blown rose,
Faster than chains will hold my soul to thine
Thro' joy, and grief, thro' life – unto its close.

We have only these tantalizing fragments to hint at the directions Chopin's work might have taken if *The Awakening* had been a critical success or even a *succès de scandale*, and if her career had not been cut off by her early death. The fate of *The Awakening* shows only too well how a literary tradition may be enabling, even essential, as well as confining. Struggling to escape from tradition, Kate Chopin courageously risked social and literary ostracism. It is up to contemporary readers to restore her solitary book to its place in our literary heritage.

Elaine Showalter

SELECT BIBLIOGRAPHY

BIOGRAPHY
Destined to become the standard biography is Emily Toth's monumental *Kate Chopin: A Solitary Soul*, Atheneum, New York, 1989. Per Seyersted's earlier *Kate Chopin: A Critical Biography*, Louisiana State University Press, Louisiana, 1969, offers a full-bodied treatment of Chopin's life but does not include material that has only recently become available. Before that there is Daniel S. Rankin's *Kate Chopin and Her Creole Stories*, University of Pennsylvania Press, Philadelphia, 1932, which paints a rather more traditional picture of Chopin's life as dutiful wife and mother when compared to the biographies of Toth and Seyersted who try to draw out the tensions between self and society as exhibited in Chopin's life and works.

GENERAL CRITICISM
Barbara C. Ewell's *Kate Chopin*, Ungar, New York, 1986, attempts to chart a path through Chopin's work as a whole, treating *The Awakening* as an inevitable climax and full-stop. Useful also to the serious student is Seyersted's critical biography mentioned above.

'THE AWAKENING'
The Awakening has received far more attention than Chopin's output as a whole. All of the works cited above have substantial chapters on the novel and there are also numerous compendiums of critical material. These include: *New Essays on The Awakening*, ed., Wendy Martin, Cambridge University Press, Cambridge, 1988; *Kate Chopin, The Awakening: An Authoritative Text, Contexts, Criticism*, ed., Margaret Culley, Norton, New York, 1976; and *Approaches to Teaching Kate Chopin's 'The Awakening'*, ed., Bernard Koloski, Modern Language Association, New York, 1988. *The Kate Chopin Companion*, Thomas Bonner, Jr, Greenwood Press, London, 1988, contains an excellent 'Bibliographic Essay' which has a near exhaustive list of anything and everything which has been written on, and by, Chopin including an extensive list of essays and articles on *The Awakening*.

Other works cited in the introduction to this edition are: *The Awakening*, Kate Chopin, Norton Critical Edition, New York, 1976 (contains a selection of introductory essays); *Disorderly Conduct: Visions of Gender in Victorian America*, Carroll Smith-Rosenberg, Knopf, New York, 1985; *Empire of the Mother: American Writing about Domesticity*,

Mary P. Ryan, Haworth Press, New York, 1982; *Private Woman, Public Stage: Literary Domesticity in Nineteenth-Century America*, Mary Kelley, Oxford University Press, New York, 1984; *Womanhood in America from Colonial Times to the Present*, Mary P. Ryan, Franklin Watts, New York, 1983; *Women's Fiction: A Guide to Novels by and about Women in America*, Nina Baym, Cornell University Press, Ithaca, N.Y., 1978; *Woman and the Myth*, Bell G. Chevigny, Feminist Press, Old Westbury, N.Y., 1976.

CHRONOLOGY

DATE	AUTHOR'S LIFE	LITERARY CONTEXT
1850	Katherin O'Flaherty (Kate Chopin) born on 8 February to Thomas O'Flaherty, an Irish immigrant and Eliza Faris, a Creole.	Dickens: *David Copperfield*. Hawthorne: *The Scarlet Letter*. Turgenev: *A Month in the Country*. Reissue of Elizabeth Barrett Browning's *Poems* in two vols. Death of Balzac (b.1799) and Wordsworth (b.1770).
1851		Elizabeth Barrett Browning: *Cassa Guida Windows*. Henry Wadsworth Longfellow: *The Golden Legend*. Hawthorne: *The House of the Seven Gables*. Herman Melville: *Moby-Dick*. Death of Mary Shelley (b.1797). Death of Fenimore Cooper (b.1789) – author of *The Last of the Mohicans*.
1851– 52		Harriet Beecher Stowe's *Uncle Tom's Cabin* serialized in the *National Era* – published in book form in 1852.
1852		
1853		Charlotte Brontë: *Villette*. Elizabeth Gaskell: *Ruth*.
1854		Birth of Sarah Grand. George Eliot publishes her translation of Feuerbach's *Essence of Christianity*.
1855	Thomas O'Flaherty (father) dies in a rail accident. Katherin begins school at St Louis Academy of the Sacred Heart.	Elizabeth Gaskell: *North and South*. Anthony Trollope: *The Warden*. Longfellow: *Hiawatha*. Walt Whitman: *Leaves of Grass*. Death of Charlotte Brontë (b.1816).

Presidential election in which the main issue is the fugitive slave law. Democrat, Franklin Pierce wins. His victory spells the end of the Whig Party. Louis Napoleon proclaimed Emperor of France.

Formation of the Republican Party in Wisconsin. Kansas-Nebraska Act, dividing Nebraska into two – this granted the right to popular sovereignty in determining the status of slavery. Crimean War (to 1856).

DATE	AUTHOR'S LIFE	LITERARY CONTEXT
1856		Births of Freud and George Bernard Shaw.
		Beecher Stowe: *Dred: A Tale of the Dismal Swamp*.
		Elizabeth Barrett Browning: *Aurora Leigh*.
		Charlotte Brontë: *The Professor*.
1857		Dickens: *Little Dorrit*.
		Flaubert: *Madame Bovary*.
		Baudelaire: *Les Fleurs du Mal*.
1858		George Eliot: *Scenes of Clerical Life*.
		Longfellow: *The Courtship of Miles Standish*.
		Emily Dickinson said to be collating her poems into 'facicles' from around this time onwards.
		Birth of Beatrice Webb.
1859		George Eliot: *Adam Bede*.
		Birth of John Dewey.
		Beecher Stowe: *The Minister's Wooing*.
		Death of Washington Irving (b.1783) – author of *Rip Van Winkle*.
1860		Wilkie Collins: *The Woman in White*.
		George Eliot: *The Mill on the Floss*.
		Elizabeth Barrett Browning: *Poems before Congress*.
		Hawthorne: *The Marble Faun*.
1861	'Kate' is confirmed by Archbishop Kendrick in May.	George Eliot: *Silas Marner*.
		Rebecca Harding Davis: *Life in the Iron Mills*.
		Harriet Davies: *Incidents in the Life of a Slave Girl*.
		Death of Elizabeth Barrett Browning (b.1806).
1862		Elizabeth Barrett Browning: *Last Poems* (published posthumously).
		Birth of Edith Wharton.

CHRONOLOGY

Democrat, James Buchanan, elected president (to 1861). Buchanan is the last Democrat to win the presidency for 24 years.

In England the Matrimonial Causes Act makes divorce available without Act of Parliament but on unequal terms for men and women.

Fenian Brotherhood founded in USA. Spreads to Ireland in early 1860s. Birth of Emily Pankhurst.

John Brown, abolitionist, leads a crowd who seize the US arsenal at Harpers Ferry, Viriginia. The government sends forces under Colonel Robert E. Lee who capture Brown. Brown is tried for treason and murder, and hanged. Charles Darwin: *The Origin of Species*.

Republicans nominate Abraham Lincoln on a platform which denounces slavery as evil, denying the right of Congress to give legality to slavery in any territory. South Carolina secedes on the slavery question in response to Lincoln.

Ten more states secede from Union on the slavery issue. In his inauguration address Lincoln affirms that he does not intend to interfere with slavery where it already exists. Lincoln makes a call for 75,000 troops with the aim of forcing the states back into the Union. Thus begins The Civil War (to 1865) and the Battle of Bull Run which is the first real clash between the Southern and Northern States – Union forces are completely routed, retreating as far as Washington. Lincoln elected President (to 1865). England declares itself neutral in the conflict.
Battle of Shiloh – Union forces successful, forcing a Confederate retreat.
Battle of Antietam in which 23,000 are left dead on the field. Lincoln proposes that slaves in all states in rebellion against the government should be free on or after 1 January 1863.

DATE	AUTHOR'S LIFE	LITERARY CONTEXT
1863	Deaths of Victoire Verdon Charleville (great-grandmother) and George O'Flaherty (half-brother) a Confederate soldier.	Elizabeth Gaskell: *Sylvia's Lovers*. Longfellow: *Tales of a Wayside Inn*.
1864		Lucie Duff Gordon: *Letters from the Cape*. Death of Nathaniel Hawthorne (b.1804).
1865	Attends the Academy of the Visitation, then returns to Sacred Heart Academy.	Elizabeth Gaskell: *Mr Harrison's Confessions* and *Wives and Daughters*. Lewis Carroll: *Alice's Adventures in Wonderland*. Death of Elizabeth Gaskell (b.1810).
1866		
1867		Birth of Laura Ingalls Wilder, author of the *Little House* series.
1868	Kate graduates from the Academy; keeps commonplace book from 1867–1870.	Louisa May Alcott: *Little Women*, the publication of which allowed her to achieve financial security.
1869	Visits New Orleans, Louisiana, in the spring for three weeks. Writes 'Emancipation: A Life Fable' afterwards. Learns to smoke.	J. S. Mill: *The Subjection of Women*. Beecher Stowe: *Old Town Folks*. Death of Lucie Duff Gordon.
1870	Marries Oscar Chopin on 9 June in Holy Angels Church, St Louis. Travels on honeymoon to Europe, visiting Germany, Switzerland and France. Oscar's mother, Julia Benoist, dies in April; his father in November. The couple move to New Orleans in October, settling in Magazine Street.	Death of Charles Dickens. Beecher Stowe writes *Lady Byron Vindicated* in which she charges Byron with incestuous relations with his half-sister.
1871	The first of Kate's six children, Jean Chopin, born on 22 May.	Walt Whitman: *Democratic Vistas*. Lewis Carroll: *Through the Looking Glass*.

CHRONOLOGY

Greatest battle of the war fought at Gettysburg, Pennsylvania. Colonel Robert E. Lee, now a commander in the Confederate Army, is forced to retreat. The Battle of Gettysburg is said to be the turning point of the war. Lincoln's 'Gettysburg Address'.
Lincoln re-nominated for president. He wins an easy victory.

Assassination of Lincoln. Andrew Johnson president to 1869. Civil War ends. A general pardon is granted to the South. Congress passes a Bill for the appointment of a committee whose function is to enquire into the question of slavery in the South. Negroes given full rights as citizens in the 14th Amendment. No State can come back into the Union unless it ratifies this amendment.
First Women's Suffrage Committee formed in Manchester.
Young Women's Christian Association formed in Boston to help city working women.
Petition requesting the franchise signed by 1,500 women, in Britain, and presented by John Stuart Mill to the House of Commons.

Ulysses S. Grant, ablest of Union generals, elected president. Suez Canal opens. Union Pacific railroad completed. Rockefeller's Standard Oil Company begins to corner the market. The West is opened up. There follows mass cultivation of land, an ever expanding frontier and population growth through immigration. These factors spell the end of the 'Wild West'.

DATE	AUTHOR'S LIFE	LITERARY CONTEXT
1872		George Eliot: *Middlemarch*. Susan Coolidge: *What Katy Did*.
1873	Oscar Chopin born. Kate's brother, Thomas O'Flaherty killed in a buggy accident.	
1874	Chopins move into the Garden District of New Orleans. Visit Grand Isle during the summer. George Chopin born.	
1876	Frederich Chopin born.	Henry James: *Roderick Hudson*. Mark Twain: *Tom Sawyer*. George Eliot: *Daniel Deronda*.
1877		Elizabeth Stuart Phelps: *The Story of Avis*. Henry James: *The American*. Tolstoy: *Anna Karenina*. Birth of Gertrude Stein.
1878	Felix Chopin born.	
1879	Chopins move to Clouterville, Louisiana after Oscar's cotton business does badly. Lelia Chopin born.	George Washington Cable: *Old Creole Days*.
1880		Birth of Marie Stopes, pioneer birth control campaigner. Death of George Eliot (b.1819).
1881		Henry James: *The Portrait of a Lady*. George M. Beard: *American Nervousness*. Deaths of Dostoevsky and Carlyle.
1882	Oscar (Kate's husband) dies of swamp fever.	Mark Twain: *The Prince and the Pauper*. William Dean Howells: *A Modern Instance*. Walt Whitman: *Specimen Days in America*. Births of Virginia Woolf and James Joyce. Death of Longfellow (b.1807).
1883		Mark Twain: *Life on the Mississippi*. Henry James: *Portraits of Places* (travel sketches).

CHRONOLOGY

Grant wins office for a second time.

A. Graham Bell invents the telephone. Edison invents the phonograph. Death of Wild Bill Hickok (b.1837) – Western folk-hero.

Presidency of Rutherford B. Hayes (to 1881).

Standard Oil refines 95% of nation's oil. Invention of the incandescent lamp. 1880s: growth of Women's clubs in cities; labour unrest – almost 10,000 strikes and lock-outs; rise of magazines – *Cosmopolitan*, the *Ladies' Home Journal*, *McClure's*; electricity for private houses; rise of department stores. Taylor's 'time-study' experiments.
Presidency of James Garfield. Garfield assassinated. Presidency of Chester Arthur (to 1885). Founding of the American Federation of Labor. Tsar Alexander II assassinated.

Jesse James shot and killed. First central power plant in New York (Edison, backed by J. P. Morgan). Birth of Sylvia Pankhurst.

DATE	AUTHOR'S LIFE	LITERARY CONTEXT
1884	Kate moves to St Louis.	Mark Twain: *Huckleberry Finn.* Maupassant: *Une Vie.*
1885	Eliza O'Flaherty, Kate's mother, dies in June. Dr Frederick Kohlbenheyer, her obstetrician, becomes Kate's confidant.	Frances Hodgson Burnett: *Little Lord Fauntleroy.* Marx: *Das Kapital II.* Howells: *The Rise of Silas Lapham.* Maupassant: *Bel-Ami.*
1886		Henry James: *The Bostonians* and *Princess Cassamassima.* Death of the American poet, Emily Dickinson (b.1830), who published only seven poems out of nearly 2,000 in her lifetime.
1887	Kate visits Natchitoches Parish (Cane River County).	
1888	Begins literary career by writing the poem 'If It Might Be' and begins the story 'Euphraisie' (unfinished). Reads Maupassant, inspiring her to write 'life, not fiction'.	Birth of Katherine Mansfield. Death of Louisa May Alcott.
1889	'If It Might Be' published in *America* (Chicago) on 16 January, her first work in print. Two stories, 'Wiser than a God' and 'A Point at Issue' published in *Post-Dispatch.*	
1890	*At Fault* (a novel) published privately – 1,000 copies. Throughout the 1890s Chopin is part of the St Louis literary and publishing circle.	Henry James: *The Tragic Muse.* William James: *Principles of Psychology.*
1891	*Young Dr Gosse* (novel manuscript later destroyed) submitted unsuccessfully to publishers.	Hardy: *Tess of the D'Urbervilles.* George Gissing: *The Odd Women* and *New Grub Street.* Dewey: *Critical Theory of Ethics.* Beatrice Webb: *The Co-operative Movement in Great Britain.* Death of Herman Melville (b.1819). US International Copyright Bill improves authors' finances.

CHRONOLOGY

Presidency of Glover Cleveland (to 1889).

The 'Great Upheaval': 700,000 on strike in the US. Demand for eight-hour day.

Benjamin Harrison, Republican, elected president (to 1893). Jane Addams establishes Hull Settlement House, Chicago.

Census: US population: 63 millions. Enumerators instructed to distinguish between 'blacks', 'mulattoes', 'quadroons' and 'octoroons'. New constitution of the state of Mississippi prohibits interracial union (the prohibition stands for 75 years). Depression: drastic fall in agricultural prices.

DATE	AUTHOR'S LIFE	LITERARY CONTEXT
1892		Charlotte Perkins Gilman: *The Yellow Wallpaper*. Stephen Crane: *Maggie: A Girl of the Streets*. Death of Walt Whitman (b.1819).
1893	'Désirée's Baby' published in *Vogue* on 4 January. Kate travels to the East of America visiting Boston with the aim of finding a publisher for a 'collection of Creole stories'.	Sarah Grand achieves sensational success with *The Heavenly Twins* which attacked the double standards in marriage. This novel launched her on a career as a 'New Woman' – a phrase she is said to have coined in 1894.
1894	*Bayou Folk* (23 stories and sketches) published. 'The Story of an Hour' written. Attends Indiana Conference of Western Association of Writers. Writes 'The Western Association of Writers' which receives hostile response. First national profile of Chopin in *The Writer*.	George Moore: *Esther Waters*. Beatrice Webb collaborates on *History of Trade Unionism* with Sidney Webb, her husband. Eliza Gamble: *The Evolution of Women*. Mark Twain: *Pudd'enhead Wilson*. Death of Christina Rossetti (b.1830).
1895	'Athénaïse' written, published in 1896.	Crane: *The Red Badge of Courage*.
1896		Sarah Orne Jewett: *The Country of the Pointed Firs*. Thomas Hardy: *Jude the Obscure*. Chekhov: *The Seagull*. Birth of Vera Brittain.
1897	*A Night in Acadie* (21 stories) published. Begins work on *The Awakening* in June. Meets Ruth McEnery Stuart.	Sarah Grand: *The Beth Book*. Beatrice Webb collaborates with her husband on *Industrial Democracy*.
1898	Chopin cited as one of the four leading literary figures in St Louis by the *Star-Times*. 'The Storm' written. Finishes *The Awakening* in January.	

HISTORICAL EVENTS

Financier Jay Gould dies worth $77 million.

New Zealand women secure the right to vote. World Columbian Exposition, Chicago. Cleveland regains office as president (to 1897).

Beginning of Freudian psychoanalysis. The USA becomes the leading manufacturing nation in the world.

William McKinley elected US President.

Klondike Gold Rush. Formation of the Women's Institute in Canada. Loie Fuller dances in New York.

Curies discover radium. Invention of the cash register. Rockefeller 'retires', *c.* $420 million. Spanish-American War.

DATE	AUTHOR'S LIFE	LITERARY CONTEXT
1899	*The Awakening* published. Offensive reviews and local displeasure with the novel affect Kate personally. She travels to Wisconsin.	Charlotte Perkins Gilman: *Women and Economics*. Thorstein Veblan: *The Theory of the Leisure Class*. Olive Schreiner: *The Women Question*. Henry James: *The Awkward Age*. Frank Norris: *McTeague*. Birth of Ernest Hemingway. Edith Wharton: *The Greater Inclination* (stories).
1900	'The Gentleman from New Orleans' written. Appears in first edition of *Who's Who* in USA.	Joseph Conrad: *Lord Jim*. Theodore Dreiser: *Sister Carrie*. Sigmund Freud: *The Interpretation of Dreams*. Edith Wharton: *The Touchstone* (novel). Deaths of Ruskin (b.1819), Nietzsche (b.1844) and Oscar Wilde (b.1854).
1901		Thomas Mann: *Buddenbrooks*. First Nobel Prize Winner for Literature.
1902		Henry James: *The Wings of the Dove*. Gide: *The Immoralist*. William James: *Varieties of Religious Experience*. Birth of John Steinbeck.
1903	Though ill, Kate moves the family residence to 4232 McPherson Avenue.	Henry James: *The Ambassadors*. Jack London: *The Call of the Wild*. G. E. Moore: *Principia Ethica*. Joseph Conrad: *Typhoon*. Dewey: *Studies in Logical Theory*. Birth of George Orwell.
1904	Kate visits St Louis World's Fair where she is stricken by a cerebral haemorrhage. She dies two days later on 20 August.	Henry James: *The Golden Bowl*. Joseph Conrad: *Nostromo*.

CHRONOLOGY

Florence Kelly (women's activist) becomes president of National Consumers' League. Outbreak of Boer War.

Planck's quantum theory. First Zeppelin flight. US population 76 million. US railroad network just under 200,000 miles.

Death of Queen Victoria; accession of Edward VII. Marconi transmits messages across the Atlantic. Theodore Roosevelt elected President of the US.
Women in Australia are granted the vote.

Women's Trade Union League founded in New York. Strengthening of immigration selection. Wright Brothers' first successful powered flight.

Emmeline Pankhurst's militant 'suffragettes': Women's social and Political Union. Theodore Roosevelt re-elected president.

THE AWAKENING

I

A green and yellow parrot, which hung in a cage outside the door, kept repeating over and over:

'*Allez vous-en! Allez vous-en! Sapristi!*[1] That's all right!'

He could speak a little Spanish, and also a language which nobody understood, unless it was the mocking bird that hung on the other side of the door, whistling his fluty notes out upon the breeze with maddening persistence.

Mr Pontellier, unable to read his newspaper with any degree of comfort, arose with an expression and an exclamation of disgust. He walked down the gallery and across the narrow 'bridges' which connected the Lebrun cottages one with the other. He had been seated before the door of the main house. The parrot and the mocking bird were the property of Madame Lebrun, and they had the right to make all the noise they wished. Mr Pontellier had the privilege of quitting their society when they ceased to be entertaining.

He stopped before the door of his own cottage, which was the fourth one from the main building and next to the last. Seating himself in a wicker

1 'Get out! Get out! Damn it!

I

rocker which was there, he once more applied himself to the task of reading the newspaper. The day was Sunday; the paper was a day old. The Sunday papers had not yet reached Grand Isle. He was already acquainted with the market reports, and he glanced restlessly over the editorials and bits of news which he had not had time to read before quitting New Orleans the day before.

Mr Pontellier wore eye glasses. He was a man of forty, of medium height and rather slender build; he stooped a little. His hair was brown and straight, parted on one side. His beard was neatly and closely trimmed.

Once in a while he withdrew his glance from the newspaper and looked about him. There was more noise than ever over at the house. The main building was called 'the house,' to distinguish it from the cottages. The chattering and whistling birds were still at it. Two young girls, the Farival twins, were playing a duet from 'Zampa' upon the piano. Madame Lebrun was bustling in and out, giving orders in a high key to a yard boy whenever she got inside the house, and directions in an equally high voice to a dining room servant whenever she got outside. She was a fresh, pretty woman, clad always in white with elbow sleeves. Her starched skirts crinkled as she came and went. Farther down, before one of the cottages, a lady in black was walking demurely up and down, telling her beads. A good many persons of the *pension* had gone over to the *Chênière Caminada*[2] in Beaudelet's lugger to hear mass. Some young people were out under the water oaks playing croquet. Mr Pontellier's two children were there – sturdy little fellows of four and five. A quadroon nurse followed them about with a far-away, meditative air.

Mr Pontellier finally lit a cigar and began to smoke, letting the paper drag idly from his hand. He fixed his gaze upon a white sunshade that was advancing at snail's pace from the beach. He could see it plainly between the gaunt trunks of the water oaks and across the stretch of yellow camomile. The gulf looked far away, melting hazily into the blue of the horizon. The sunshade continued to approach slowly. Beneath its pink-lined shelter were his wife, Mrs Pontellier, and young Robert Lebrun. When they reached the cottage, the two seated themselves with some appearance of fatigue upon the upper step of the porch, facing each other, each leaning against a supporting post.

'What folly! to bathe at such an hour in such heat!' exclaimed Mr Pontellier. He himself had taken a plunge at daylight. That was why the morning seemed long to him.

'You are burnt beyond recognition,' he added, looking at his wife as one looks at a valuable piece of personal property which has suffered some damage. She held up her hands, strong, shapely

2 An island covered with live oaks, named after the bay situated in the southern end of Jefferson parish, where Grand Isle is also located.

hands, and surveyed them critically, drawing up her lawn sleeves above the wrists. Looking at them reminded her of her rings, which she had given to her husband before leaving for the beach. She silently reached out to him, and he, understanding, took the rings from his vest pocket and dropped them into her open palm. She slipped them upon her fingers; then clasping her knees, she looked across at Robert and began to laugh. The rings sparkled upon her fingers. He sent back an answering smile.

'What is it?' asked Pontellier, looking lazily and amused from one to the other. It was some utter nonsense; some adventure out there in the water, and they both tried to relate it at once. It did not seem half so amusing when told. They realized this, and so did Mr Pontellier. He yawned and stretched himself. Then he got up, saying he had half a mind to go over to Klein's hotel and play a game of billiards.

'Come go along, Lebrun,' he proposed to Robert. But Robert admitted quite frankly that he preferred to stay where he was and talk to Mrs Pontellier.

'Well, send him about his business when he bores you, Edna,' instructed her husband as he prepared to leave.

'Here, take the umbrella,' she exclaimed, holding it out to him. He accepted the sunshade, and lifting it over his head descended the steps and walked away.

'Coming back to dinner?' his wife called after

him. He halted a moment and shrugged his shoulders. He felt in his vest pocket; there was a ten-dollar bill there. He did not know; perhaps he would return for the early dinner and perhaps he would not. It all depended upon the company which he found over at Klein's and the size of 'the game.' He did not say this, but she understood it, and laughed, nodding good-by to him.

Both children wanted to follow their father when they saw him starting out. He kissed them and promised to bring them back bonbons and peanuts.

II

Mrs Pontellier's eyes were quick and bright; they were a yellowish brown, about the color of her hair. She had a way of turning them swiftly upon an object and holding them there as if lost in some inward maze of contemplation or thought.

Her eyebrows were a shade darker than her hair. They were thick and almost horizontal, emphasizing the depth of her eyes. She was rather handsome than beautiful. Her face was captivating by reason of a certain frankness of expression and a contradictory subtle play of features. Her manner was engaging.

Robert rolled a cigarette. He smoked cigarettes because he could not afford cigars, he said. He had a cigar in his pocket which Mr Pontellier had presented him with and he was saving it for his afterdinner smoke.

This seemed quite proper and natural on his part. In coloring he was not unlike his companion. A clean-shaved face made the resemblance more pronounced that it would otherwise have been. There rested no shadow of care upon his open countenance. His eyes gathered in and reflected the light and languor of the summer day.

Mrs Pontellier reached over for a palm-leaf fan

that lay on the porch and began to fan herself, while Robert sent between his lips light puffs from his cigarette. They chatted incessantly: about the things around them; their amusing adventure out in the water – it had again assumed its entertaining aspect; about the wind, the trees, the people who had gone to the *Chênière*; about the children playing croquet under the oaks, and the Farival twins, who were now performing the overture to 'The Poet and the Peasant.'

Robert talked a good deal about himself. He was very young, and did not know any better. Mrs Pontellier talked a little about herself for the same reason. Each was interested in what the other said. Robert spoke of his intention to go to Mexico in the autumn, where fortune awaited him. He was always intending to go to Mexico, but some way never got there. Meanwhile he held on to his modest position in a mercantile house in New Orleans, where an equal familiarity with English, French and Spanish gave him no small value as a clerk and correspondent.

He was spending his summer vacation, as he always did, with his mother at Grand Isle. In former times, before Robert could remember, 'the house' had been a summer luxury of the Lebruns. Now, flanked by its dozen or more cottages, which were always filled with exclusive visitors from the *Quartier Français*,' it enabled Madame Lebrun to maintain the easy and comfortable existence which appeared to be her birthright.

Mrs Pontellier talked about her father's Mississippi plantation and her girlhood home in the old Kentucky bluegrass country. She was an American woman, with a small infusion of French which seemed to have been lost in dilution. She read a letter from her sister, who was away in the East, and who had engaged herself to be married. Robert was interested, and wanted to know what manner of girls the sisters were, what the father was like, and how long the mother had been dead.

When Mrs Pontellier folded the letter it was time for her to dress for the early dinner.

'I see Léonce isn't coming back,' she said, with a glance in the direction whence her husband had disappeared. Robert supposed he was not, as there were a good many New Orleans club men over at Klein's.

When Mrs Pontellier left him to enter her room, the young man descended the steps and strolled over toward the croquet players, where, during the half-hour before dinner, he amused himself with the little Pontellier children, who were very fond of him.

III

It was eleven o'clock that night when Mr Pontellier returned from Klein's hotel. He was in an excellent humor, in high spirits, and very talkative. His entrance awoke his wife, who was in bed and fast asleep when he came in. He talked to her while he undressed, telling her anecdotes and bits of news and gossip that he had gathered during the day. From his trousers pockets he took a fistful of crumpled bank notes and a good deal of silver coin, which he piled on the bureau indiscriminately with keys, knife, handkerchief, and whatever else happened to be in his pockets. She was overcome with sleep, and answered him with little half utterances.

He thought it very discouraging that his wife who was the sole object of his existence, evinced so little interest in things which concerned him, and valued so little his conversation.

Mr Pontellier had forgotten the bonbons and peanuts for the boys. Notwithstanding he loved them very much, and went into the adjoining room where they slept to take a look at them and make sure that they were resting comfortably. The result of his investigation was far from satisfactory. He turned and shifted the youngsters about in bed.

One of them began to kick and talk about a basket full of crabs.

Mr Pontellier returned to his wife with the information that Raoul had a high fever and needed looking after. Then he lit a cigar and went and sat near the open door to smoke it.

Mrs Pontellier was quite sure Raoul had no fever. He had gone to bed perfectly well, she said, and nothing had ailed him all day. Mr Pontellier was too well acquainted with fever symptoms to be mistaken. He assured her the child was consuming at that moment in the next room.

He reproached his wife with her inattention, her habitual neglect of the children. If it was not a mother's place to look after children, whose on earth was it? He himself had his hands full with his brokerage business. He could not be in two places at once; making a living for his family on the street, and staying at home to see that no harm befell them. He talked in a monotonous, insistent way.

Mrs Pontellier sprang out of bed and went into the next room. She soon came back and sat on the edge of the bed, leaning her head down on the pillow. She said nothing, and refused to answer her husband when he questioned her. When his cigar was smoked out he went to bed, and in half a minute he was fast asleep.

Mrs Pontellier was by that time thoroughly awake. She began to cry a little, and wiped her eyes on the sleeve of her *peignoir*. Blowing out the candle, which her husband had left burning, she slipped her bare

feet into a pair of satin *mules* at the foot of the bed
and went out on the porch, where she sat down in
the wicker chair and began to rock gently to and
fro.

It was then past midnight. The cottages were all
dark. A single faint light gleamed out from the
hallway of the house. There was no sound abroad
except the hooting of an old owl in the top of a
water-oak, and the everlasting voice of the sea, that
was not uplifted at that soft hour. It broke like a
mournful lullaby upon the night.

The tears came so fast to Mrs Pontellier's eyes
that the damp sleeve of her *peignoir* no longer served
to dry them. She was holding the back of her chair
with one hand; her loose sleeve had slipped almost
to the shoulder of her uplifted arm. Turning, she
thrust her face, steaming and wet, into the bend of
her arm, and she went on crying there, not caring
any longer to dry her face, her eyes, her arms. She
could not have told why she was crying. Such
experiences as the foregoing were not uncommon
in her married life. They seemed never before to
have weighed much against the abundance of her
husband's kindness and a uniform devotion which
had come to be tacit and self-understood.

An indescribable oppression, which seemed to
generate in some unfamiliar part of her consciousness, filled her whole being with a vague anguish. It
was like a shadow, like a mist passing across her
soul's summer day. It was strange and unfamiliar; it
was a mood. She did not sit there inwardly upbraid-

ing her husband, lamenting at Fate, which had directed her footsteps to the path which they had taken. She was just having a good cry all to herself. The mosquitoes made merry over her, biting her firm, round arms and nipping at her bare insteps.

The little stinging, buzzing imps succeeded in dispelling a mood which might have held her there in the darkness half a night longer.

The following morning Mr Pontellier was up in good time to take the rockaway[3] which was to convey him to the steamer at the wharf. He was returning to the city to his business, and they would not see him again at the Island till the coming Saturday. He had regained his composure, which seemed to have been somewhat impaired the night before. He was eager to be gone, as he looked forward to a lively week in Carondelet Street.[4]

Mr Pontellier gave his wife half of the money which he had brought away from Klein's hotel the evening before. She liked money as well as most women, and accepted it with no little satisfaction.

'It will buy a handsome wedding present for Sister Janet!' she exclaimed, smoothing out the bills as she counted them one by one.

'Oh! we'll treat Sister Janet better than that, my dear,' he laughed, as he prepared to kiss her good-by.

3 A light, low, four-wheeled carriage with a standing top, open at the sides; so named because originally manufactured in Rockaway, New Jersey.
4 At one time an important center of business in New Orleans.

The boys were tumbling about, clinging to his legs, imploring that numerous things be brought back to them. Mr Pontellier was a great favorite, and ladies, men, children, even nurses, were always on hand to say good-by to him. His wife stood smiling and waving, the boys shouting, as he disappeared in the old rockaway down the sandy road.

A few days later a box arrived for Mrs Pontellier from New Orleans. It was from her husband. It was filled with *friandises*,[5] with luscious and toothsome bits – the finest of fruits, *patés*, a rare bottle or two, delicious syrups, and bonbons in abundance.

Mrs Pontellier was always very generous with the contents of such a box; she was quite used to receiving them when away from home. The *patés* and fruit were brought to the dining-room; the bonbons were passed around. And the ladies, selecting with dainty and discriminating fingers and a little greedily, all declared that Mr Pontellier was the best husband in the world. Mrs Pontellier was forced to admit that she knew of none better.

5 Delicacies.

IV

It would have been a difficult matter for Mr Pontellier to define to his own satisfaction or any one else's wherein his wife failed in her duty toward their children. It was something which he felt rather than perceived, and he never voiced the feeling without subsequent regret and ample atonement.

If one of the little Pontellier boys took a tumble whilst at play, he was not apt to rush crying to his mother's arms for comfort; he would more likely pick himself up, wipe the water out of his eyes and the sand out of his mouth, and go on playing. Tots as they were, they pulled together and stood their ground in childish battles with doubled fists and uplifted voices, which usually prevailed against the other mother-tots. The quadroon nurse was looked upon as a huge encumbrance, only good to button up waists and panties and to brush and part hair; since it seemed to be a law of society that hair must be parted and brushed.

In short, Mrs Pontellier was not a mother-woman. The mother-women seemed to prevail that summer at Grand Isle. It was easy to know them, fluttering about with extended, protecting wings when any harm, real or imaginary, threatened their precious brood. They were women who idolized their children, worshiped their husbands, and esteemed it a holy privilege to efface themselves as individuals and grow wings as ministering angels.

Many of them were delicious in the rôle; one of them was the embodiment of every womanly grace and charm. If her husband did not adore her, he was a brute, deserving of death by slow torture. Her name was Adèle Ratignolle. There are no words to describe her save the old ones that have served so often to picture the bygone heroine of romance and the fair lady of our dreams. There was nothing subtle or hidden about her charms; her beauty was all there, flaming and apparent: the spun-gold hair that comb nor confining pin could restrain; the blue eyes that were like nothing but sapphires; two lips that pouted, that were so red one could only think of cherries or some other delicious crimson fruit in looking at them. She was growing a little stout, but it did not seem to detract an iota from the grace of every step, pose, gesture. One would not have wanted her white neck a mite less full or her beautiful arms more slender. Never were hands more exquisite than hers, and it was a joy to look at them when she threaded her needle or adjusted her gold thimble to her taper middle finger as she sewed away on the little night-drawers or fashioned a bodice or a bib.

Madame Ratignolle was very fond of Mrs Pontellier, and often she took her sewing and went over to sit with her in the afternoons. She was sitting there the afternoon of the day the box arrived from New

Orleans. She had possession of the rocker, and she was busily engaged in sewing upon a diminutive pair of night-drawers.

She had brought the pattern of the drawers for Mrs Pontellier to cut out – a marvel of construction, fashioned to enclose a baby's body so effectually that only two small eyes might look out from the garment, like an Eskimo's. They were designed for winter wear, when treacherous drafts came down chimneys and insidious currents of deadly cold found their way through keyholes.

Mrs Pontellier's mind was quite at rest concerning the present material needs of her children, and she could not see the use of anticipating and making winter night garments the subject of her summer meditations. But she did not want to appear unamiable and uninterested, so she had brought forth newspapers, which she spread upon the floor of the gallery, and under Madame Ratignolle's directions she had cut a pattern of the impervious garment.

Robert was there, seated as he had been the Sunday before, and Mrs Pontellier also occupied her former position on the upper step, leaning listlessly against the post. Beside her was a box of bonbons, which she held out at intervals to Madame Ratignolle.

That lady seemed at a loss to make a selection, but finally settled upon a stick of nougat, wondering if it were not too rich; whether it could possibly hurt her. Madame Ratignolle had been married seven years. About every two years she had a baby. At that time she had three babies, and was beginning to think of a fourth one. She was always talking about her 'condition.' Her 'condition' was in no way apparent, and no one would have known a thing about it but for her persistence in making it the subject of conversation.

Robert started to reassure her, asserting that he had known a lady who had subsisted upon nougat during the entire – but seeing the color mount into Mrs Pontellier's face he checked himself and changed the subject.

Mrs Pontellier, though she had married a Creole, was not thoroughly at home in the society of Creoles; never before had she been thrown so intimately among them. There were only Creoles that summer at Lebrun's. They all knew each other, and felt like one large family, among whom existed the most amicable relations. A characteristic which distinguished them and which impressed Mrs Pontellier most forcibly was their entire absence of prudery. Their freedom of expression was at first incomprehensible to her, though she had no difficulty in reconciling it with a lofty chastity which in the Creole woman seems to be inborn and unmistakable.

Never would Edna Pontellier forget the shock with which she heard Madame Ratignolle relating to old Monsieur Farival the harrowing story of one of her *accouchements*, withholding no intimate detail. She was growing accustomed to like shocks, but she could not keep the mounting color back from her cheeks. Oftener than once her coming had interrupted the droll story with which Robert was entertaining some amused group of married women.

A book had gone the rounds of the *pension*. When it came her turn to read it, she did so with profound astonishment. She felt moved to read the book in secret and solitude, though none of the others had done so – to hide it from view at the sound of approaching footsteps. It was openly criticised and freely discussed at table. Mrs Pontellier gave over being astonished, and concluded that wonders would never cease.

V

They formed a congenial group sitting there that summer afternoon – Madame Ratignolle sewing away, often stopping to relate a story or incident with much expressive gesture of her perfect hands; Robert and Mrs Pontellier sitting idle, exchanging occasional words, glances or smiles which indicated a certain advanced stage of intimacy and *camaraderie*.

He had lived in her shadow during the past month. No one thought anything of it. Many had predicted that Robert would devote himself to Mrs Pontellier when he arrived. Since the age of fifteen, which was eleven years before, Robert each summer at Grand Isle had constituted himself the devoted attendant of some fair dame or damsel. Sometimes it was a young girl, again a widow; but as often as not it was some interesting married woman.

For two consecutive seasons he lived in the sunlight of Mademoiselle Duvigné's presence. But she died between summers; then Robert posed as an inconsolable, prostrating himself at the feet of Madame Ratignolle for whatever crumbs of sympathy and comfort she might be pleased to vouchsafe.

Mrs Pontellier liked to sit and gaze at her fair

companion as she might look upon a faultless Madonna.

'Could any one fathom the cruelty beneath that fair exterior?' murmured Robert. 'She knew that I adored her once, and she let me adore her. It was "Robert, come; go; stand up; sit down; do this; do that; see if the baby sleeps; my thimble, please, that I left God knows where. Come and read Daudet to me while I sew."

'*Par exemple*! I never had to ask. You were always there under my feet, like a troublesome cat.'

'You mean like an adoring dog. And just as soon as Ratignolle appeared on the scene, then it *was* like a dog. "*Passez! Adieu! Allez vous-en!*" '[6]

'Perhaps I feared to make Alphonse jealous,' she interjoined, with excessive naïveté. That made them all laugh. The right hand jealous of the left! The heart jealous of the soul! But for that matter, the Creole husband is never jealous; with him the gangrene passion is one which has become dwarfed by disuse.

Meanwhile Robert, addressing Mrs Pontellier, continued to tell of his one time hopeless passion for Madame Ratignolle; of sleepless nights, of consuming flames till the very sea sizzled when he took his daily plunge. While the lady at the needle kept up a little running, contemptuous comment:

'*Blagueur – farceur – gros bête, va!*'[7]

He never assumed this serio-comic tone when

6 Get along! Good-by! Out with you!
7 Hoaxer – jokester – great beast, go!

alone with Mrs Pontellier. She never knew precisely what to make of it; at that moment it was impossible for her to guess how much of it was jest and what proportion was earnest. It was understood that he had often spoken words of love to Madame Ratignolle, without any thought of being taken seriously. Mrs Pontellier was glad he had not assumed a similar rôle toward herself. It would have been unacceptable and annoying.

Mrs Pontellier had brought her sketching materials, which she sometimes dabbled with in an unprofessional way. She liked the dabbling. She felt in it satisfaction of a kind which no other employment afforded her.

She had long wished to try herself on Madame Ratignolle. Never had that lady seemed a more tempting subject than at that moment, seated there like some sensuous Madonna, with the gleam of the fading day enriching her splendid color.

Robert crossed over and seated himself upon the step below Mrs Pontellier, that he might watch her work. She handled her brushes with a certain ease and freedom which came, not from long and close acquaintance with them, but from a natural aptitude. Robert followed her work with close attention, giving forth little ejaculatory expressions of appreciation in French, which he addressed to Madame Ratignolle.

'*Mais ce n'est pas mal! Elle s'y connait, elle a de la force, oui.*'[8]

8 But it's not bad. She knows what she's doing, she has ability, hasn't she?

During his oblivious attention he once quietly rested his head against Mrs Pontellier's arm. As gently she repulsed him. Once again he repeated the offense. She could not but believe it to be thoughtlessness on his part, yet that was no reason she should submit to it. She did not remonstrate, except again to repulse him quietly but firmly. He offered no apology.

The picture completed bore no resemblance to Madame Ratignolle. She was greatly disappointed to find that it did not look like her. But it was a fair enough piece of work, and in many respects satisfying.

Mrs Pontellier evidently did not think so. After surveying the sketch critically she drew a broad smudge of paint across its surface, and crumpled the paper between her hands.

The youngsters came tumbling up the steps, the quadroon following at the respectful distance which they required her to observe. Mrs Pontellier made them carry her paints and things into the house. She sought to detain them for a little talk and some pleasantry. But they were greatly in earnest. They had only come to investigate the contents of the bonbon box. They accepted without murmuring what she chose to give them, each holding out two chubby hands scoop-like, in the vain hope that they might be filled; and then away they went.

The sun was low in the west, and the breeze soft and languorous that came up from the south, charged with the seductive odor of the sea. Children, freshly befurbelowed, were gathering for their games under the oaks. Their voices were high and penetrating.

Madame Ratignolle folded her sewing, placing thimble, scissors and thread all neatly together in the roll, which she pinned securely. She complained of faintness. Mrs Pontellier flew for the cologne water and a fan. She bathed Madame Ratignolle's face with cologne, while Robert plied the fan with unnecessary vigor.

The spell was soon over, and Mrs Pontellier could not help wondering if there were not a little imagination responsible for its origin, for the rose tint had never faded from her friend's face.

She stood watching the fair woman walk down the long line of galleries[9] with the grace and majesty which queens are sometimes supposed to possess. Her little ones ran to meet her. Two of them clung about her white skirts, the third she took from its nurse and with a thousand endearments bore it along in her own fond, encircling arms. Though, as everybody well knew, the doctor had forbidden her to lift so much as a pin!

'Are you going bathing?' asked Robert of Mrs Pontellier. It was not so much a question as a reminder.

'Oh, no,' she answered, with a tone of indecision. 'I'm tired; I think not.' Her glance wandered from his face away toward the Gulf, whose sonorous

9 Balconies or verandas.

murmur reached her like a loving but imperative entreaty.

'Oh, come!' he insisted. 'You mustn't miss your bath. Come on. The water must be delicious; it will not hurt you. Come.'

He reached up for her big, rough straw hat that hung on a peg outside the door, and put it on her head. They descended the steps, and walked away together toward the beach. The sun was low in the west and the breeze was soft and warm.

VI

Edna Pontellier could not have told why, wishing to go to the beach with Robert, she should in the first place have declined, and in the second place have followed in obedience to one of the the two contradictory impulses which impelled her.

A certain light was begining to dawn dimly within her – the light which, showing the way, forbids it.

At that early period it served but to bewilder her. It moved her to dreams, to thoughtfulness, to the shadowy anguish which had overcome her the midnight when she had abandoned herself to tears.

In short, Mrs Pontellier was beginning to realize her position in the universe as a human being, and to recognize her relations as an individual to the world within and about her. This may seem like a ponderous weight of wisdom to descend upon the soul of a young woman of twenty-eight – perhaps more wisdom than the Holy Ghost is usually pleased to vouchsafe to any woman.

But the beginning of things, of a world especially, is necessarily vague, tangled, chaotic, and exceedingly disturbing. How few of us ever emerge from such beginning! How many souls perish in its tumult!

The voice of the sea is seductive; never ceasing,

whispering, clamoring, murmuring, inviting the soul to wander for a spell in abysses of solitude; to lose itself in mazes of inward contemplation.

The voice of the sea speaks to the soul. The touch of the sea is sensuous, enfolding the body in its soft, close embrace.

VII

Mrs Pontellier was not a woman given to confidences, a characteristic hitherto contrary to her nature. Even as a child she had lived her own small life all within herself. At a very early period she had apprehended instinctively the dual life – that outward existence which conforms, the inward life which questions.

That summer at Grand Isle she began to loosen a little the mantle of reserve that had always enveloped her. There may have been – there must have been – influences, both subtle and apparent, working in their several ways to induce her to do this; but the most obvious was the influence of Adèle Ratignolle. The excessive physical charm of the Creole had first attracted her, for Edna had a sensuous susceptibility to beauty. Then the candor of the woman's whole existence, which every one might read, and which formed so striking a contrast to her own habitual reserve – this might have furnished a link. Who can tell what metals the gods use in forging the subtle bond which we call sympathy, which we might as well call love.

The two women went away one morning to the beach together, arm in arm, under the huge white sunshade. Edna had prevailed upon Madame Ratignolle to leave the children behind, though she could not induce her to relinquish a diminutive roll of needlework, which Adèle begged to be allowed to slip into the depths of her pocket. In some unaccountable way they had escaped from Robert.

The walk to the beach was no inconsiderable one, consisting as it did of a long, sandy path, upon which a sporadic and tangled growth that bordered it on either side made frequent and unexpected inroads. There were acres of yellow camomile reaching out on either hand. Further away still, vegetable gardens abounded, with frequent small plantations of orange or lemon trees intervening. The dark green clusters glistened from afar in the sun.

The women were both of goodly height, Madame Ratignolle possessing the more feminine and matronly figure. The charm of Edna Pontellier's physique stole insensibly upon you. The lines of her body were long, clean and symmetrical; it was a body which occasionally fell into splendid poses; there was no suggestion of the trim, stereotyped fashion-plate about it. A casual and indiscriminating observer, in passing, might not cast a second glance upon the figure. But with more feeling and discernment he would have recognized the noble beauty of its modeling, and the graceful severity of poise and movement, which made Edna Pontellier different from the crowd.

She wore a cool muslin that morning – white, with a waving vertical line of brown running through it; also a white linen collar and the big straw hat which she had taken from the peg outside the door. The hat rested any way on her yellow-brown hair, that waved a little, was heavy, and clung close to her head.

Madame Ratignolle, more careful of her complexion, had twined a gauze veil about her head. She wore doeskin gloves, with gauntlets that protected her wrists. She was dressed in pure white, with a fluffiness of ruffles that became her. The draperies and fluttering things which she wore suited her rich, luxuriant beauty as a greater severity of line could not have done.

There were a number of bath-houses along the beach, of rough but solid construction, built with small, protecting galleries facing the water. Each house consisted of two compartments, and each family at Lebrun's possessed a compartment for itself, fitted out with all the essential paraphernalia of the bath and whatever other conveniences the owners might desire. The two women had no intention of bathing; they had just strolled down to the beach for a walk and to be alone and near the water. The Pontellier and Ratignolle compartments adjoined one another under the same roof.

Mrs Pontellier had brought down her key through force of habit. Unlocking the door of her bath-room she went inside, and soon emerged, bringing a rug, which she spread upon the floor of the gallery, and two huge hair pillows covered with crash, which she placed against the front of the building.

The two seated themselves there in the shade of the porch, side by side, with their backs against the pillows and their feet extended. Madame Ratignolle removed her veil, wiped her face with a rather delicate handkerchief, and fanned herself with the fan which she always carried suspended somewhere about her person by a long, narrow ribbon. Edna removed her collar and opened her dress at the throat. She took the fan from Madame Ratignolle and began to fan both herself and her companion. It was very warm, and for a while they did nothing but exchange remarks about the heat, the sun, the glare. But there was a breeze blowing, a choppy, stiff wind that whipped the water into froth. It fluttered the skirts of the two women and kept them for a while engaged in adjusting, readjusting, tucking in, securing hair-pins and hatpins. A few persons were sporting some distance away in the water. The beach was very still of human sound at that hour. The lady in black was reading her morning devotions on the porch of a neighboring bath-house. Two young lovers were exchanging their hearts' yearnings beneath the children's tent, which they had found unoccupied.

Edna Pontellier, casting her eyes about, had finally kept them at rest upon the sea. The day was clear and carried the gaze out as far as the blue sky went; there were a few white clouds suspended idly over the horizon. A lateen sail was visible in the direction of Cat Island, and others to the south seemed almost motionless in the far distance.

'Of whom – of what are you thinking?' asked Adèle of her companion, whose countenance she had been watching with a little amused attention, arrested by the absorbed expression which seemed to have seized and fixed every feature into a statuesque repose.

'Nothing,' returned Mrs Pontellier, with a start, adding at once: 'How stupid! But it seems to me it is the reply we make instinctively to such a question. Let me see,' she went on, throwing back her head and narrowing her fine eyes till they shone like two vivid points of light. 'Let me see. I was really not conscious of thinking of anything, but perhaps I can retrace my thoughts.'

'Oh! never mind!' laughed Madame Ratignolle. 'I am not quite so exacting. I will let you off this time. It is really too hot to think, especially to think about thinking.'

'But for the fun of it,' persisted Edna. 'First of all, the sight of the water stretching so far away, those motionless sails against the blue sky, made a delicious picture that I just wanted to sit and look at. The hot wind beating in my face made me think – without any connection that I can trace – of a summer day in Kentucky, of a meadow that seemed as big as the ocean to the very little girl walking through the grass, which was higher than her waist. She threw out her arms as if swimming when she walked, beating the tall grass as one strikes out in the water. Oh, I see the connection now!'

'Where were you going that day in Kentucky, walking through the grass?'

'I don't remember now. I was just walking diagonally across a big field. My sunbonnet obstructed the view. I could see only the stretch of green before me, and I felt as if I must walk on forever, without coming to the end of it. I don't remember whether I was frightened or pleased. I must have been entertained.

'Likely as not it was Sunday,' she laughed; 'and I was running away from prayers, from the Presbyterian service, read in a spirit of gloom by my father that chills me yet to think of.'

'And have you been running away from prayers ever since, *ma chère*?' asked Madame Ratignolle, amused.

'No! oh, no!' Edna hastened to say. 'I was a little unthinking child in those days, just following a misleading impulse without question. On the contrary, during one period of my life religion took a firm hold upon me; after I was twelve and until – until – why, I suppose until now, though I never thought much about it – just driven along by habit. But do you know,' she broke off, turning her quick eyes upon Madame Ratignolle and leaning forward a little so as to bring her face quite close to that of her companion, 'sometimes I feel this summer as if I were walking through the green meadow again, idly, aimlessly, unthinking and unguided.'

Madame Ratignolle laid her hand over that of Mrs Pontellier, which was near her. Seeing that the hand was not withdrawn, she clasped it firmly and warmly. She even stroked it a little, fondly, with the other hand, murmuring in an undertone, '*Pauvre chérie.*'

The action was at first a little confusing to Edna, but she soon lent herself readily to the Creole's gentle caress. She was not accustomed to an outward and spoken expression of affection, either in herself or in others. She and her younger sister, Janet, had quarreled a good deal through force of unfortunate habit. Her older sister, Margaret, was matronly and dignified, probably from having assumed matronly and housewifely responsibilities too early in life, their mother having died when they were quite young. Margaret was not effusive; she was practical. Edna had had an occasional girl friend, but whether accidentally or not, they seemed to have been all of one type – the self-contained. She never realized that the reserve of her own character had much, perhaps everything, to do with this. Her most intimate friend at school had been one of rather exceptional intellectual gifts, who wrote fine-sounding essays, which Edna admired and strove to imitate; and with her she talked and glowed over the English classics, and sometimes held religious and political controversies.

Edna often wondered at one propensity which sometimes had inwardly disturbed her without causing any outward show or manifestation on her part. At a very early age – perhaps it was when she traversed the ocean of waving grass – she remembered that she had been passionately enamoured of a dignified and sad-eyed cavalry officer who visited her father in Kentucky. She could not leave his presence when he was there, nor remove her eyes from his face, which was something like Napoleon's, with a lock of black hair falling across the forehead. But the cavalry officer melted imperceptibly out of her existence.

At another time her affections were deeply engaged by a young gentleman who visited a lady on a neighboring plantation. It was after they went to Mississippi to live. The young man was engaged to be married to the young lady, and they sometimes called upon Margaret, driving over of afternoons in a buggy. Edna was a little miss, just merging into her teens; and the realization that she herself was nothing, nothing, nothing to the engaged young man was a bitter affliction to her. But he, too, went the way of dreams.

She was a grown woman when she was overtaken by what she supposed to be the climax of her fate. It was when the face and figure of a great tragedian began to haunt her imagination and stir her senses. The persistence of the infatuation lent it an aspect of genuineness. The hopelessness of it colored it with the lofty tones of a great passion.

The picture of the tragedian stood enframed upon her desk. Any one may possess the portrait of a tragedian without exciting suspicion or comment. (This was a sinister reflection which she cherished.) In the presence of others she expressed admiration

34

for his exalted gifts, as she handed the photograph around and dwelt upon the fidelity of the likeness. When alone she sometimes picked it up and kissed the cold glass passionately.

Her marriage to Léonce Pontellier was purely an accident, in this respect resembling many other marriages which masquerade as the decrees of Fate. It was in the midst of her secret great passion that she met him. He fell in love, as men are in the habit of doing, and pressed his suit with an earnestness and an ardor which left nothing to be desired. He pleased her; his absolute devotion flattered her. She fancied there was a sympathy of thought and taste between them, in which fancy she was mistaken. Add to this the violent opposition of her father and her sister Margaret to her marriage with a Catholic, and we need seek no further for the motives which led her to accept Monsieur Pontellier for her husband.

The acme of bliss, which would have been a marriage with the tragedian, was not for her in this world. As the devoted wife of a man who worshipped her, she felt she would take her place with a certain dignity in the world of reality, closing the portals forever behind her upon the realm of romance and dreams.

But it was not long before the tragedian had gone to join the cavalry officer and the engaged young man and a few others; and Edna found herself face to face with the realities. She grew fond of her husband, realizing with some unaccountable satisfaction that no trace of passion or excessive and fictitious warmth colored her affection, thereby threatening its dissolution.

She was fond of her children in an uneven, impulsive way. She would sometimes gather them passionately to her heart; she would sometimes forget them. The year before they had spent part of the summer with their grandmother Pontellier in Iberville. Feeling secure regarding their happiness and welfare, she did not miss them except with an occasional intense longing. Their absence was a sort of relief, though she did not admit this, even to herself. It seemed to free her of a responsibility which she had blindly assumed and for which Fate had not fitted her.

Edna did not reveal so much as all this to Madame Ratignolle that summer day when they sat with faces turned to the sea. But a good part of it escaped her. She had put her head down on Madame Ratignolle's shoulder. She was flushed and felt intoxicated with the sound of her own voice and the unaccustomed taste of candor. It muddled her like wine, or like a first breath of freedom.

There was the sound of approaching voices. It was Robert, surrounded by a troop of children, searching for them. The two little Pontelliers were with him, and he carried Madame Ratignolle's little girl in his arms. There were other children besides, and two nursemaids followed, looking disagreeable and resigned.

The women at once rose and began to shake out

their draperies and relax their muscles. Mrs Pontellier threw the cushions and rug into the bath-house.
The children all scampered off to the awning, and
they stood there in a line, gazing upon the intruding
lovers, still exchanging their vows and sighs. The
lovers got up, with only a silent protest, and walked
slowly away somewhere else.

The children possessed themselves of the tent,
and Mrs Pontellier went over to join them.

Madame Ratignolle begged Robert to accompany
her to the house; she complained of cramp in her
limbs and stiffness of the joints. She leaned drag-
gingly upon his arm as they walked.

VIII

'Do me a favor, Robert,' spoke the pretty woman at his side, almost as soon as she and Robert had started on their slow, homeward way. She looked up in his face, leaning on his arm beneath the encircling shadow of the umbrella which he had lifted.

'Granted; as many as you like,' he returned, glancing down into her eyes that were full of thoughtfulness and some speculation.

'I only ask for one; let Mrs Pontellier alone.'

'*Tiens!*' he exclaimed, with a sudden, boyish laugh. '*Voilà que Madame Ratignolle est jalouse!*'[10]

'Nonsense! I'm in earnest; I mean what I say. Let Mrs Pontellier alone.'

'Why?' he asked; himself growing serious at his companion's solicitation.

'She is not one of us; she is not like us. She might make the unfortunate blunder of taking you seriously.'

His face flushed with annoyance, and taking off his soft hat he began to beat it impatiently against his leg as he walked. 'Why shouldn't she take me seriously?' he demanded sharply. 'Am I a comedian,

10 Can it be that Madame Ratignolle is jealous?

a clown, a jack-in-the-box? Why shouldn't she? You Creolcs! I have no patience with you! Am I always to be regarded as a fcature of an amusing pro-gramme? I hope Mrs Pontellier does take me seriously. I hope she has discernment enough to find in me something besides the *blagueur*.[11] If I thought there was any doubt – '

'Oh, enough, Robert!' she broke into his heated outburst, 'You are not thinking of what you are saying. You speak with as little reflection as we might expect from one of those children down there playing in the sand. If your attentions to any married women here were ever offered with any intention of being convincing, you would not be the gentleman we all know you to be, and you would be unfit to associate with the wives and daughters of the people who trust you.'

Madame Ratignolle had spoken what she believed to be the law and the gospel. The young man shrugged his shoulders impatiently.

'Oh! well! That isn't it,' slamming his hat down vehemently upon his head. 'You ought to feel that such things are not flattering to say to a fellow.'

'Should our whole intercourse consist of an exchange of compliments? *Ma foi!*'[12]

'It isn't pleasant to have a woman tell you – ' he went on, unheedingly, but breaking off suddenly: 'Now if I were like Arobin – you remember Alcée

11 Braggart; a pretentious fellow.
12 Indeed! Literally, My faith!

Arobin and that story of the consul's wife at Biloxi?' And he related the story of Alcée Arobin and the consul's wife, and another about the tenor of the French Opera, who received letters which should never have been written, and still other stories, grave and gay, till Mrs Pontellier and her possible propensity for taking young men seriously was apparently forgotten.

Madame Ratignolle, when they had regained her cottage, went in to take the hour's rest which she considered helpful. Before leaving her, Robert begged her pardon for the impatience – he called it rudeness – with which he had received her well-meant caution.

'You made one mistake, Adèle,' he said, with a light smile; 'there is no earthly possibility of Mrs Pontellier ever taking me seriously. You should have warned me against taking myself seriously. Your advice might then have carried some weight and given me subject for some reflection. *Au revoir.* But you look tired,' he added solicitously. 'Would you like a cup of bouillon? Shall I stir you a toddy? Let me mix you a toddy with a drop of Angostura.'

She acceded to the suggestion of bouillon, which was grateful and acceptable. He went himself to the kitchen, which was a building apart from the cottages and lying to the rear of the house. And he himself brought her the golden-brown bouillon, in a dainty Sèvres cup, with a flaky cracker or two on the saucer.

She thrust a bare, white arm from the curtain

which shielded her open door, and received the cup from his hands. She told him he was a *bon garçon*, and she meant it. Robert thanked her and turned away toward 'the house.'

The lovers were just entering the grounds of the *pension*. They were leaning toward each other as the water oaks bent from the sea. There was not a particle of earth beneath their feet. Their heads might have been turned upside down, so absolutely did they tread upon blue ether. The lady in black, creeping behind them, looked a trifle paler and more jaded than usual. There was no sign of Mrs Pontellier and the children. Robert scanned the distance for any such apparition. They would doubtless remain away till the dinner hour. The young man ascended to his mother's room. It was situated at the top of the house, made up of odd angles and a queer, sloping ceiling. Two broad dormer windows looked out toward the Gulf, and as far across it as a man's eye might reach. The furnishings of the room were light, cool, and practical.

Madame Lebrun was busily engaged at the sewing machine. A little black girl sat on the floor, and with her hands worked the treadle of the machine. The Creole woman does not take any chances which may be avoided of imperiling her health.

Robert went over and seated himself on the broad sill of one of the dormer windows. He took a book from his pocket and began energetically to read it, judging by the precision and frequency with which he turned the leaves. The sewing machine made a resounding clatter in the room; it was a ponderous, bygone make. In the lulls, Robert and his mother exchanged bits of desultory conversation.

'Where is Mrs Pontellier?'

'Down at the beach with the children.'

'I promised to lend her the Goncourt. Don't forget to take it down when you go; it's there on the bookshelf over the small table.' Clatter, clatter, clatter, bang! for the next five or eight minutes.

'Where is Victor going with the rockaway?'

'The rockaway? Victor?'

'Yes, down there in front. He seems to be getting ready to drive away somewhere.'

'Call him.' Clatter, clatter!

Robert uttered a shrill, piercing whistle which might have been heard back at the wharf.

'He won't look up.'

Madame Lebrun flew to the window. She called 'Victor!' She waved a handkerchief and called again. The young fellow below got into the vehicle and started the horse off at a gallop.

Madame Lebrun went back to the machine, crimson with annoyance. Victor was the younger son and brother – a *tête montée*,[13] with a temper which invited violence and a will which no ax could break.

'Whenever you say the word I'm ready to thrash

13 An excitable and willful fellow.

any amount of reason into him that he's able to hold.'

'If your father had only lived!' Clatter, clatter, clatter clatter, bang! It was a fixed belief with Madame Lebrun that the conduct of the universe and all things pertaining thereto would have been manifestly of a more intelligent and higher order had not Monsieur Lebrun been removed to other spheres during the early years of their married life.

'What do you hear from Montel?' Montel was a middle-aged gentleman whose vain ambition and desire for the past twenty years had been to fill the void which Monsieur Lebrun's taking off had left in the Lebrun household. Clatter, clatter, bang, clatter!

'I have a letter somewhere,' looking in the machine drawer and finding the letter in the bottom of the workbasket. 'He says to tell you he will be in Vera Cruz the beginning of next month' – clatter, clatter! – 'and if you still have the intention of joining him' – bang! clatter clatter, bang!

'Why didn't you tell me so before, mother? You know I wanted – ' Clatter, clatter, clatter!

'Do you see Mrs Pontellier starting back with the children? She will be in late to luncheon again. She never starts to get ready for luncheon till the last minute.' Clatter, clatter! 'Where are you going?'

'Where did you say the Goncourt was?'

IX

Every light in the hall was ablaze, every lamp turned as high as it could be without smoking the chimney or threatening explosion. The lamps were fixed at intervals against the wall, encircling the whole room. Some one had gathered orange and lemon branches, and with these fashioned graceful festoons between. The dark green of the branches stood out and glistened against the white muslin curtains which draped the windows, and which puffed, floated, and flapped at the capricious will of a stiff breeze that swept up from the Gulf.

It was Saturday night a few weeks after the intimate conversation between Robert and Madame Ratignolle on their way from the beach. An unusual number of husbands, fathers, and friends had come down to stay over Sunday, and they were being suitably entertained by their families, with the material help of Madame Lebrun. The dining tables had all been removed to one end of the hall, and the chairs ranged about in rows and in clusters. Each little family group had had its say and exchanged its domestic gossip earlier in the evening. There was now an apparent disposition to relax, to widen the circle of confidences and give a more general tone to the conversation.

Many of the children had been permitted to sit up beyond their usual bedtime. A small band of them were lying on their stomachs on the floor looking at the colored sheets of the comic papers which Mr Pontellier had brought down. The little Pontellier boys were permitting them to do so, and making their authority felt.

Music, dancing, and a recitation or two were the entertainments furnished, or rather, offered. But there was nothing systematic about the programme, no appearance of prearrangement nor even premeditation.

At an early hour in the evening the Farival twins were prevailed upon to play the piano. They were girls of fourteen, always clad in the Virgin's colors, blue and white, having been dedicated to the Blessed Virgin at their baptism. They played a duet from 'Zampa,' and at the earnest solicitation of everyone present followed it with the overture to 'The Poet and the Peasant.'

'*Allez vous-en! Sapristi!*' shrieked the parrot outside the door. He was the only being present who possessed sufficient candor to admit that he was not listening to these gracious performances for the first time that summer. Old Monsieur Farival, grandfather of the twins, grew indignant over the interruption, and insisted upon having the bird removed and consigned to regions of darkness. Victor Lebrun objected, and his decrees were as immutable as those of Fate. The parrot fortunately offered no further interruption to the entertainment, the whole venom of his nature apparently having been cherished up and hurled against the twins in that one impetuous outburst.

Later a young brother and sister gave recitations, which everyone present had heard many times at winter evening entertainments in the city.

A little girl performed a skirt dance in the center of the floor. The mother played her accompaniments and at the same time watched her daughter with greedy admiration and nervous apprehension. She need have had no apprehension. The child was mistress of the situation. She had been properly dressed for the occasion in black tulle and black silk tights. Her little neck and arms were bare, and her hair, artificially crimped, stood out like fluffy black plumes over her head. Her poses were full of grace, and her little black-shod toes twinkled as they shot out and upward with a rapidity and suddenness which were bewildering.

But there was no reason why everyone should not dance. Madame Ratignolle could not, so it was she who gaily consented to play for the others. She played very well, keeping excellent waltz time and infusing an expression into the strains which was indeed inspiring. She was keeping up her music on account of the children, she said, because she and her husband both considered it a means of brightening the home and making it attractive.

Almost everyone danced but the twins, who could not be induced to separate during the brief period when one or the other should be whirling around the room in the arms of a man. They might have danced together, but they did not think of it.

The children were sent to bed. Some went submissively; others with shrieks and protests as they were dragged away. They had been permitted to sit up till after the ice cream, which naturally marked the limit of human indulgence.

The ice cream was passed around with cake – gold and silver cake arranged on platters in alternate slices; it had been made and frozen during the afternoon at the back of the kitchen by two black women, under the supervision of Victor. It was pronounced a great success – excellent if it had only contained a little less vanilla or a little more sugar, if it had been frozen a degree harder, and if the salt might have been kept out of portions of it. Victor was proud of his achievement, and went about recommending it and urging everyone to partake of it to excess.

After Mrs Pontellier had danced twice with her husband, once with Robert, and once with Monsieur Ratignolle, who was thin and tall and swayed like a reed in the wind when he danced, she went out on the gallery and seated herself on the low window sill, where she commanded a view of all that went on in the hall and could look out toward the Gulf. There was a soft effulgence in the east. The moon was coming up, and its mystic shimmer was casting a million lights across the distant, restless water.

'Would you like to hear Mademoiselle Reisz play?' asked Robert, coming out on the porch where she was. Of course Edna would like to hear Mademoiselle Reisz play; but she feared it would be useless to entreat her.

'I'll ask her,' he said. 'I'll tell her that you want to hear her. She likes you. She will come.' He turned and hurried away to one of the far cottages, where Mademoiselle Reisz was shuffling away. She was dragging a chair in and out of her room, and at intervals objecting to the crying of a baby, which a nurse in the adjoining cottage was endeavoring to put to sleep. She was a disagreeable little woman, no longer young, who had quarreled with almost everyone, owing to a temper which was self-assertive and a disposition to trample upon the rights of others. Robert prevailed upon her without any too great difficulty.

She entered the hall with him during a lull in the dance. She made an awkward, imperious little bow as she went in. She was a homely woman, with a small weazened face and body and eyes that glowed. She had absolutely no taste in dress, and wore a batch of rusty black lace with a bunch of artificial violets pinned to the side of her hair.

'Ask Mrs Pontellier what she would like to hear me play,' she requested of Robert. She sat perfectly still before the piano, not touching the keys, while Robert carried her message to Edna at the window. A general air of surprise and genuine satisfaction fell upon everyone as they saw the pianist enter. There was a settling down, and a prevailing air of expectancy everywhere. Edna was a trifle embarrassed at being thus signaled out for the imperious little woman's favor. She would not dare to choose, and begged that Mademoiselle Reisz would please herself in her selections.

Edna was what she herself called very fond of music. Musical strains, well rendered, had a way of evoking pictures in her mind. She sometimes liked to sit in the room of mornings when Madame Ratignolle played or practised. One piece which that lady played Edna had entitled 'Solitude.' It was a short, plaintive, minor strain. The name of the piece was something else, but she called it 'Solitude.' When she heard it there came before her imagination the figure of a man standing beside a desolate rock on the seashore. He was naked. His attitude was one of hopeless resignation as he looked toward a distant bird winging its flight away from him.

Another piece called to her mind a dainty young woman clad in an Empire gown, taking mincing dancing steps as she came down a long avenue between tall hedges. Again, another reminded her of children at play, and still another of nothing on earth but a demure lady stroking a cat.

The very first chords which Mademoiselle Reisz struck upon the piano sent a keen tremor down Mrs Pontellier's spinal column. It was not the first time she had heard an artist at the piano. Perhaps it was the first time she was ready, perhaps the first time her being was tempered to take an impress of the abiding truth.

She waited for the material pictures which she thought would gather and blaze before her imagination. She waited in vain. She saw no pictures of solitude, of hope, of longing, or of despair. But the very passions themselves were aroused within her soul, swaying it, lashing it, as the waves daily beat upon her splendid body. She trembled, she was choking, and the tears blinded her.

Mademoiselle had finished. She arose, and bowing her stiff, lofty bow, she went away, stopping for neither thanks nor applause. As she passed along the gallery she patted Edna upon the shoulder.

'Well, how did you like my music?' she asked. The young woman was unable to answer; she pressed the hand of the pianist convulsively. Mademoiselle Reisz perceived her agitation and even her tears. She patted her again upon the shoulder as she said:

'You are the only one worth playing for. Those others? Bah!' and she went shuffling and sidling on down the gallery toward her room.

But she was mistaken about 'those others.' Her playing had aroused a fever of enthusiasm. 'What passion!' 'What an artist!' 'I have always said no one could play Chopin like Mademoiselle Reisz!' 'That last prelude! Bon Dieu! It shakes a man!'

It was growing late, and there was a general disposition to disband. But some one, perhaps it was Robert, thought of a bath at that mystic hour and under that mystic moon.

X

At all events Robert proposed it, and there was not a dissenting voice. There was not one but was ready to follow whcn he led the way. He did not lead the way, however, he directed the way; and he himself loitered behind with the lovers, who had betrayed a disposition to linger and hold themselves apart. He walked between them, whether with malicious or mischievous intent was not wholly clear, even to himself.

The Pontelliers and Ratignolles walked ahead; the women leaning upon the arms of their husbands. Edna could hear Robert's voice behind them, and could sometimes hear what he said. She wondered why he did not join them. It was unlike him not to. Of late he had sometimes held away from her for an entire day, redoubling his devotion upon the next and the next, as though to make up for hours that had been lost. She missed him the days when some pretext served to take him away from her, just as one misses the sun on a cloudy day without having thought much about the sun when it was shining.

The people walked in little groups toward the beach. They talked and laughed; some of them sang. There was a band playing down at Klein's hotel, and the strains reached them faintly, tempered by the distance. There were strange, rare odors abroad – a tangle of the sea smell and of weeds and damp, new-plowed earth, mingled with the heavy perfume of a field of white blossoms somewhere near. But the night sat lightly upon the sea and the land. There was no weight of darkness; there were no shadows. The white light of the moon had fallen upon the world like the mystery and the softness of sleep.

Most of them walked into the water as though into a native element. The sea was quiet now, and swelled lazily in broad billows that melted into one another and did not break except upon the beach in little foamy crests that coiled back like slow, white serpents.

Edna had attempted all summer to learn to swim. She had received instructions from both the men and women, in some instances from the children. Robert had pursued a system of lessons almost daily, and he was nearly at the point of discouragement in realizing the futility of his efforts. A certain ungovernable dread hung about her when in the water, unless there was a hand near by that might reach out and reassure her.

But that night she was like the little tottering, stumbling, clutching child, who of a sudden realizes its powers, and walks for the first time alone, boldy and with overconfidence. She could have shouted for joy. She did shout for joy, as with a sweeping stroke or two she lifted her body to the surface of the water.

A feeling of exultation overtook her, as if some power of significant import had been given her to control the working of her body and her soul. She grew daring and reckless, overestimating her strength. She wanted to swim far out, where no woman had swum before.

Her unlooked-for achievement was the subject of wonder, applause, and admiration. Each one congratulated himself that his special teachings had accomplished this desired end.

'How easy it is!' she thought. 'It is nothing,' she said aloud; 'why did I not discover before that it was nothing. Think of the time I have lost splashing about like a baby!' She would not join the groups in their sports and bouts, but intoxicated with her newly conquered power, she swam out alone.

She turned her face seaward to gather in an impression of space and solitude, which the vast expanse of water, meeting and melting with the moonlit sky, conveyed to her excited fancy. As she swam she seemed to be reaching out for the unlimited in which to lose herself.

Once she turned and looked toward the shore, toward the people she had left there. She had not gone any great distance – that is, what would have been a great distance for an experienced swimmer. But to her unaccustomed vision the stretch of water behind her assumed the aspect of a barrier which her unaided strength would never be able to overcome.

A quick vision of death smote her soul, and for a

second of time appalled and enfeebled her senses. But by an effort she rallied her staggering faculties and managed to regain the land.

She made no mention of her encounter with death and her flash of terror, except to say to her husband, 'I thought I should have perished out there alone.'

'You were not so very far, my dear; I was watching you,' he told her.

Edna went at once to the bath-house, and she had put on her dry clothes and was ready to return home before the others had left the water. She started to walk away alone. They all called to her and shouted to her. She waved a dissenting hand, and went on, paying no further heed to their renewed cries which sought to detain her.

'Sometimes I am tempted to think that Mrs Pontellier is capricious,' said Madame Lebrun, who was amusing herself immensely and feared that Edna's abrupt departure might put an end to the pleasure.

'I know she is,' assented Mr Pontellier, 'sometimes, not often.'

Edna had not traversed a quarter of the distance on her way home before she was overtaken by Robert.

'Did you think I was afraid?' she asked him, without a shade of annoyance.

'No; I knew you weren't afraid.'

'Then why did you come? Why didn't you stay out there with the others?'

'I never thought of it.'

'Thought of what?'

'Of anything. What difference does it make?'

'I'm very tired,' she uttered, complainingly.

'I know you are.'

'You don't know anything about it. Why should you know? I never was so exhausted in my life. But it isn't unpleasant. A thousand emotions have swept through me tonight. I don't comprehend half of them. Don't mind what I'm saying; I am just thinking aloud. I wonder if I shall ever be stirred again as Mademoiselle Reisz's playing moved me tonight. I wonder if any night on earth will ever again be like this one. It is like a night in a dream. The people about me are like some uncanny, half-human beings. There must be spirits abroad tonight.'

'There are,' whispered Robert. 'Didn't you know this was the twenty-eighth of August?'

'The twenty-eighth of August?'

'Yes. On the twenty-eighth of August, at the hour of midnight, and if the moon is shining – the moon must be shining – a spirit that has haunted these shores for ages rises up from the Gulf. With its own penetrating vision the spirit seeks some one mortal worthy to hold him company, worthy of being exalted for a few hours into realms of the semicelestials. His search has always hitherto been fruitless, and he has sunk back, disheartened, into the sea. But tonight he found Mrs Pontellier. Perhaps he will never wholly release her from the spell. Perhaps she will never again suffer a poor, unworthy earthling to walk in the shadow of her divine presence.'

'Don't banter me,' she said, wounded at what appeared to be his flippancy. He did not mind the entreaty, but the tone with its delicate note of pathos was like a reproach. He could not explain; he could not tell her that he had penetrated her mood and understood. He said nothing except to offer her his arm, for, by her own admission, she was exhausted. She had been walking alone with her arms hanging limp, letting her white skirts trail along the dewy path. She took his arm, but she did not lean upon it. She let her hand lie listlessly, as though her thoughts were elsewhere – somewhere in advance of her body, and she was striving to overtake them.

Robert assisted her into the hammock which swung from the post before her door out to the trunk of a tree.

'Will you stay out here and wait for Mr Pontellier?' he asked.

'I'll stay out here. Good night.'

'Shall I get you a pillow?'

'There's one here,' she said, feeling about, for they were in the shadow.

'It must be soiled; the children have been tumbling it about.'

'No matter.' And having discovered the pillow, she adjusted it beneath her head. She extended herself in the hammock with a deep breath of relief. She was not a supercilious or an over-dainty woman. She was not much given to reclining in the hammock, and when she did so it was with no catlike suggestion of voluptuous ease, but with a beneficent repose which seemed to invade her whole body.

'Shall I stay with you till Mr Pontellier comes?' asked Robert, seating himself on the outer edge of one of the steps and taking hold of the hammock rope which was fastened to the post.

'If you wish. Don't swing the hammock. Will you get my white shawl which I left on the window sill over at the house?'

'Are you chilly?'

'No; but I shall be presently.'

'Presently?' he laughed. 'Do you know what time it is? How long are you going to stay out here?'

'I don't know. Will you get the shawl?'

'Of course I will,' he said, rising. He went over to the house, walking along the grass. She watched his figure pass in and out of the strips of moonlight. It was past midnight. It was very quiet.

When he returned with the shawl she took it and kept it in her hand. She did not put it around her.

'Did you say I should stay till Mr Pontellier came back?'

'I said you might if you wished to.'

He seated himself again and rolled a cigarette, which he smoked in silence. Neither did Mrs Pontellier speak. No multitude of words could have been more significant than those moments of silence, or more pregnant with the first-felt throbbings of desire.

When the voices of the bathers were heard approaching, Robert said goodnight. She did not answer him. He thought she was asleep. Again she watched his figure pass in and out of the strips of moonlight as he walked away.

XI

'What are you doing out here, Edna? I thought I should find you in bed,' said her husband, when he discovered her lying there. He had walked up with Madame Lebrun and left her at the house. His wife did not reply.

'Are you asleep?' he asked, bending down close to look at her.

'No.' Her eyes gleamed bright and intense, with no sleepy shadows, as they looked into his.

'Do you know it is past one o'clock? Come on,' and he mounted the steps and went into their room.

'Edna!' called Mr Pontellier from within, after a few moments had gone by.

'Don't wait for me,' she answered. He thrust his head through the door.

'You will take cold out there,' he said irritably. 'What folly is this? Why don't you come in?'

'It isn't cold; I have my shawl.'

'The mosquitoes will devour you.'

'There are no mosquitoes.'

She heard him moving about the room; every sound indicating impatience and irritation. Another time she would have gone in at his request. She would, through habit, have yielded to his desire; not with any sense of submission or obedience to his compelling wishes, but unthinkingly, as we walk, move, sit, stand, go through the daily treadmill of the life which had been portioned out to us.

'Edna, dear, are you not coming in soon?' he asked again, this time fondly, with a note of entreaty.

'No; I am going to stay out here.'

'This is more than folly,' he blurted out. 'I can't permit you to stay out there all night. You must come in the house instantly.'

With a writhing motion she settled herself more securely in the hammock. She perceived that her will had blazed up, stubborn and resistant. She could not at that moment have done other than denied and resisted. She wondered if her husband had ever spoken to her like that before, and if she had submitted to his command. Of course she had; she remembered that she had. But she could not realize why or how she should have yielded, feeling as she then did.

'Léonce, go to bed,' she said. 'I mean to stay out here. I don't wish to go in, and I don't intend to. Don't speak to me like that again; I shall not answer you.'

Mr Pontellier had prepared for bed, but he slipped on an extra garment. He opened a bottle of wine, of which he kept a small and select supply in a buffet of his own. He drank a glass of the wine and went out on the gallery and offered a glass to his wife. She did not wish any. He drew up the rocker, hoisted his slippered feet on the rail, and proceeded to smoke a cigar. He smoked two cigars;

then he went inside and drank another glass of wine. Mrs Pontellier again declined to accept a glass when it was offered to her. Mr Pontellier once more seated himself with elevated feet, and after a reasonable interval of time smoked some more cigars.

Edna began to feel like one who awakens gradually out of a dream, a delicious, grotesque, impossible dream, to feel again the realities pressing into her soul. The physical need for sleep began to overtake her; the exuberance which had sustained and exalted her spirit left her helpless and yielding to the conditions which crowded her in.

The stillest hour of the night had come, the hour before dawn, when the world seems to hold its breath. The moon hung low, and had turned from silver to copper in the sleeping sky. The old owl no longer hooted, and the water-oaks had ceased to moan as they bent their heads.

Edna arose, cramped from lying so long and still in the hammock. She tottered up the steps, clutching feebly at the post before passing into the house.

'Are you coming in, Léonce?' she asked, turning her face toward her husband.

'Yes, dear,' he answered, with a glance following a misty puff of smoke. 'Just as soon as I have finished my cigar.'

XII

She slept but a few hours. They were troubled and feverish hours, disturbed with dreams that were intangible, that eluded her, leaving only an impression upon her half-awakened senses of something unattainable. She was up and dressed in the cool of the early morning. The air was invigorating and steadied somewhat her faculties. However, she was not seeking refreshment or help from any source, either external or from within. She was blindly following whatever impulse moved her, as if she had placed herself in alien hands for direction, and freed her soul of responsibility.

Most of the people at that early hour were still in bed and asleep. A few, who intended to go over to the *Chênière* for mass, were moving about. The lovers, who had laid their plans the night before, were already strolling toward the wharf. The lady in black, with her Sunday prayerbook, velvet and gold-clasped, and her Sunday silver beads, was following them at no great distance. Old Monsieur Farival was up, and was more than half inclined to do anything that suggested itself. He put on his big straw hat, and taking his umbrella from the stand in the hall, followed the lady in black, never overtaking her.

The little negro girl who worked Madame Lebrun's sewing machine was sweeping the galleries with long, absent-minded strokes of the broom. Edna sent her up into the house to awaken Robert.

'Tell him I am going to the *Chênière*. The boat is ready; tell him to hurry.

He had soon joined her. She had never sent for him before. She had never asked for him. She had never seemed to want him before. She did not appear conscious that she had done anything unusual in commanding his presence. He apparently equally unconscious of anything extraordinary in the situation. But his face was suffused with a quiet glow when he met her.

They went together back to the kitchen to drink coffee. There was no time to wait for any nicety of service. They stood outside the window and the cook passed them their coffee and a roll, which they drank and ate from the window sill. Edna said it tasted good. She had not thought of coffee nor of anything. He told her he had often noticed that she lacked forethought.

'Wasn't it enough to think of going to the *Chênière* and waking you up?' she laughed. 'Do I have to think of everything? – as Léonce says when he's in a bad humor. I don't blame him; he'd never be in a bad humor if it weren't for me.'

They took a short cut across the sands. At a distance they could see the curious procession moving toward the wharf – the lovers, shoulder to shoulder, creeping; the lady in black, gaining steadily upon them; old Monsieur Farival, losing ground inch by inch, and a young barefooted Spanish girl, with a red kerchief on her head and a basket on her arm, bringing up the rear.

Robert knew the girl, and he talked to her a little in the boat. No one present understood what they said. Her name was Mariequita. She had a round, sly, piquant face and pretty black eyes. Her hands were small, and she kept them folded over the handle of her basket. Her feet were broad and coarse. She did not strive to hide them. Edna looked at her feet, and noticed the sand and slime between her brown toes.

Beaudelet grumbled because Mariequita was there, taking up so much room. In reality he was annoyed at having old Monsieur Farival, who considered himself the better sailor of the two. But he would not quarrel with so old a man as Monsieur Farival, so he quarreled with Mariequita. The girl was deprecatory at one moment, appealing to Robert. She was saucy the next, moving her head up and down, making 'eyes' at Robert and making 'mouths' at Beaudelet.

The lovers were all alone. They saw nothing, they heard nothing. The lady in black was counting her beads for the third time. Old Monsieur Farival talked incessantly of what he knew about handling a boat, and of what Beaudelet did not know on the same subject.

Edna liked it all. She looked Mariequita up and

down, from her ugly brown toes to her pretty black eyes, and back again.

'Why does she look at me like that?' inquired the girl of Robert.

'Maybe she thinks you are pretty. Shall I ask her?'

'No. Is she your sweetheart?'

'She's a married lady, and has two children.'

'Oh! well! Francisco ran away with Sylvano's wife, who had four children. They took all his money and one of the children and stole his boat.'

'Shut up!'

'Does she understand?'

'Oh hush!'

'Are those two married over there – leaning on each other?'

'Of course not,' laughed Robert.

'Of course not,' echoed Mariequita, with a serious, confirmatory bob of the head.

The sun was high up and beginning to bite. The swift breeze seemed to Edna to bury the sting of it into the pores of her face and hands. Robert held his umbrella over her.

As they went cutting sidewise through the water, the sails bellied taut, with the wind filling and over-flowing them. Old Monsieur Farival laughed sar-donically at something as he looked at the sails, and Beaudelet swore at the old man under his breath.

Sailing across the bay to the *Chênière Caminada*, Edna felt as if she were being borne away from some anchorage which had held her fast, whose chains had been loosening – had snapped the night before when the mystic spirit was abroad, leaving her free to drift whithersoever she chose to set her sails. Robert spoke to her incessantly; he no longer noticed Mariequita. The girl had shrimps in her bamboo basket. They were covered with Spanish moss. She beat the moss down impatiently, and muttered to herself sullenly.

'Let us go to Grande Terre tomorrow?' said Robert in a low voice.

'What shall we do there?'

'Climb up the hill to the old fort and look at the little wriggling gold snakes, and watch the lizards sun themselves.'

She gazed away toward Grande Terre and thought she would like to be alone there with Robert, in the sun, listening to the ocean's roar and watching the slimy lizards writhe in and out among the ruins of the old fort.

'And the next day or the next we can sail to the Bayou Brulow,' he went on.

'What shall we do there?'

'Anything – cast bait for fish.'

'No; we'll go back to Grande Terre. Let the fish alone.'

'We'll go wherever you like,' he said. 'I'll have Tonie come over and help me patch and trim my boat. We shall not need Beaudelet nor any one. Are you afraid of the pirogue?'

'Oh, no.'

'Then I'll take you some night in the pirogue when the moon shines. Maybe your Gulf spirit will whisper to you in which of these islands the treasures are hidden – direct you to the very spot, perhaps.'

'And in a day we shall be rich!' she laughed. 'I'd give it all to you, the pirate gold and every bit of treasure we could dig up. I think you would know how to spend it. Pirate gold isn't a thing to be hoarded or utilized. It is something to squander and throw to the four winds, for the fun of seeing the golden specks fly.'

'We'd share it, and scatter it together,' he said. His face flushed.

They all went together up to the quaint little Gothic church of Our Lady of Lourdes, gleaming all brown and yellow with paint in the sun's glare.

Only Beaudelet remained behind, tinkering at his boat, and Mariequita walked away with her basket of shrimps, casting a look of childish ill-humor and reproach at Robert from the corner of her eye.

XIII

A feeling of oppression and drowsiness overcame Edna during the service. Her head began to ache, and the lights on the altar swayed before her eyes. Another time she might have made an effort to regain her composure; but her one thought was to quit the stifling atmosphere of church and reach the open air. She arose, climbing over Robert's feet with a muttered apology. Old Monsieur Farival, flurried, curious, stood up, but upon seeing that Robert had followed Mrs Pontellier, he sank back into his seat. He whispered an anxious inquiry of the lady in black, who did not notice him or reply, but kept her eyes fastened upon the pages of her velvet prayer-book.

'I felt giddy and almost overcome,' Edna said, lifting her hands instinctively to her head and pushing her straw hat up from her forehead. 'I couldn't have stayed through the service.' They were outside in the shadow of the church. Robert was full of solicitude.

'It was folly to have thought of going in the first place, let alone staying. Come over to Madame Antoine's; you can rest there.' He took her arm and led her away, looking anxiously and continuously down into her face.

How still it was, with only the voice of the sea whispering through the reeds that grew in the salt-water pools! The long line of little gray, weather-beaten houses nestled peacefully among the orange trees. It must always have been God's day on that low, drowsy island, Edna thought. They stopped, leaning over a jagged fence made of sea drift, to ask for water. A youth, a mild-faced Acadian, was drawing water from the cistern, which was nothing more than a rusty buoy, with an opening on one side, sunk in the ground. The water which the youth handed to them in a tin pail was not cold to taste, but it was cool to her heated face, and it greatly revived and refreshed her.

Madame Antoine's cot was at the far end of the village. She welcomed them with all the native hospitality, as she would have opened her door to let the sunlight in. She was fat, and walked heavily and clumsily across the floor. She could speak no English, but when Robert made her understand that the lady who accompanied him was ill and desired to rest, she was all eagerness to make Edna feel at home and to dispose of her comfortably.

The whole place was immaculately clean, and the big, four-posted bed, snow-white, invited one to repose. It stood in a small side room which looked out across a narrow grass plot toward the shed, where there was a disabled boat lying keel upward.

Madame Antoine had not gone to mass. Her son Tonie had, but she supposed he would soon be back, and she invited Robert to be seated and wait for him. But he went and sat outside the door and smoked. Madame Antoine busied herself in the large front room preparing dinner. She was boiling mullets over a few red coals in the huge fireplace.

Edna, left alone in the little side room, loosened her clothes, removing the greater part of them. She bathed her face, her neck and arms in the basin that stood between the windows. She took off her shoes and stockings and stretched herself in the very center of the high, white bed. How luxurious it felt to rest thus in a strange, quaint bed, with its sweet country odor of laurel lingering about the sheets and mattress! She stretched her strong limbs that ached a little. She ran her fingers through her loosened hair for a while. She looked at her round arms as she held them straight up and rubbed them one after the other, observing closely, as if it were something she saw for the first time, the fine, firm quality and texture of her flesh. She clasped her hands easily above her head, and it was thus she fell asleep.

She slept lightly at first, half awake and drowsily attentive to the things about her. She could hear Madame Antoine's heavy, scraping tread as she walked back and forth on the sanded floor. Some chickens were clucking outside the windows, scratching for bits of gravel in the grass. Later she half heard the voices of Robert and Tonie talking under the shed. She did not stir. Even her eyelids rested numb and heavily over her sleepy eyes. The voices went on – Tonie's slow, Acadian drawl,

70

Robert's quick, soft, smooth French. She understood French imperfectly unless directly addressed, and the voices were only part of the other drowsy, muffled sounds lulling her senses.

When Edna awoke it was with the conviction that she had slept long and soundly. The voices were hushed under the shed. Madame Antoine's step was no longer to be heard in the adjoining room. Even the chickens had gone elsewhere to scratch and cluck. The mosquito bar was drawn over her; the old woman had come in while she slept and let down the bar. Edna arose quietly from the bed, and looking between the curtains of the window, she saw by the slanting rays of the sun that the afternoon was far advanced. Robert was out there under the shed, reclining in the shade against the sloping keel of the overturned boat. He was reading from a book. Tonie was no longer with him. She wondered what had become of the rest of the party. She peeped out at him two or three times as she stood washing herself in the little basin between the windows.

Madame Antoine had laid some coarse, clean towels upon a chair, and had placed a box of *poudre de riz* within easy reach. Edna dabbed the powder upon her nose and cheeks as she looked at herself closely in the little distorted mirror which hung on the wall above the basin. Her eyes were bright and wide awake and her face glowed.

When she had completed her toilet she walked into the adjoining room. She was very hungry. No one was there. But there was a cloth spread upon the table that stood against the wall, and a cover was laid for one, with a crusty brown loaf and a bottle of wine beside the plate. Edna bit a piece from the brown loaf, tearing it with her strong, white teeth. She poured some of the wine into the glass and drank it down. Then she went softly out of doors, and plucking an orange from the low-hanging bough of a tree, threw it at Robert, who did not know she was awake and up.

An illumination broke over his whole face when he saw her and joined her under the orange tree.

'How many years have I slept?' she inquired. 'The whole island seems changed. A new race of beings must have sprung up, leaving only you and me as past relics. How many ages ago did Madame Antoine and Tonie die? and when did our people from Grand Isle disappear from the earth?'

He familiarly adjusted a ruffle upon her shoulder.

'You have slept precisely one hundred years. I was left here to guard your slumbers; and for one hundred years I have been out under the shed reading a book. The only evil I couldn't prevent was to keep a broiled fowl from drying up.'

'If it has turned to stone, still will I eat it,' said Edna, moving with him into the house. 'But really, what has become of Monsieur Farival and the others?'

'Gone hours ago. When they found that you were sleeping they thought it best not to awake you. Any way, I wouldn't have let them. What was I here for?'

'I wonder if Léonce will be uneasy!' she speculated, as she seated herself at table.

'Of course not; he knows you are with me,' Robert replied, as he busied himself among sundry pans and covered dishes which had been left standing on the hearth.

'Where are Madame Antoine and her son?' asked Edna.

'Gone to Vespers, and to visit some friends, I believe. I am to take you back in Tonie's boat whenever you are ready to go.'

He stirred the smouldering ashes till the broiled fowl began to sizzle afresh. He served her with no mean repast, dripping the coffee anew and sharing it with her. Madame Antoine had cooked little else than the mullets, but while Edna slept Robert had foraged the island. He was childishly gratified to discover her appetite, and to see the relish with which she ate the food which he had procured for her.

'Shall we go right away?' she asked, after draining her glass and brushing together the crumbs of the crusty loaf.

'The sun isn't as low as it will be in two hours,' he answered.

'The sun will be gone in two hours.'

'Well, let it go; who cares!'

They waited a good while under the orange trees, till Madame Antoine came back, panting, waddling, with a thousand apologies to explain her absence. Tonie did not dare to return. He was shy, and would not willingly face any woman except his mother.

It was very pleasant to stay there under the orange trees, while the sun dipped lower and lower, turning the western sky to flaming copper and gold. The shadows lengthened and crept out like stealthy, grotesque monsters across the grass.

Edna and Robert both sat upon the ground – that is, he lay upon the ground beside her, occasionally picking at the hem of her muslin gown.

Madame Antoine seated her fat body, broad and squat, upon a bench beside the door. She had been talking all the afternoon, and had wound herself up to the story-telling pitch.

And what stories she told them! But twice in her life she had left the *Chênière Caminada*, and then for the briefest span. All her years she had squatted and waddled there upon the island, gathering legends of the Baratarians and the sea. The night came on, with the moon to lighten it. Edna could hear the whispering voices of dead men and the click of muffled gold.

When she and Robert stepped into Tonie's boat, with the red lateen sail, misty spirit forms were prowling in the shadows and among the reeds, and upon the water were phantom ships, speeding to cover.

XIV

The youngest boy, Étienne, had been very naughty, Madame Ratignolle said, as she delivered him into the hands of his mother. He had been unwilling to go to bed and had made a scene; whereupon she had taken charge of him and pacified him as well as she could. Raoul had been in bed and asleep for two hours.

The youngster was in his long white nightgown, that kept tripping him up as Madame Ratignolle led him along by the hand. With the other chubby fist he rubbed his eyes, which were heavy with sleep and ill humor. Edna took him in her arms, and seating herself in the rocker, began to coddle and caress him, calling him all manner of tender names, soothing him to sleep.

It was not more than nine o'clock. No one had yet gone to bed but the children.

Léonce had been very uneasy at first, Madame Ratignolle said, and had wanted to start at once for the *Chênière*. But Monsieur Farival had assured him that his wife was only overcome with sleep and fatigue, that Tonie would bring her safely back later in the day; and he had thus been dissuaded from crossing the bay. He had gone over to Klein's, looking up some cotton broker whom he wished to see in regard to securities, exchanges, stocks, bonds, or something of the sort, Madame Ratignolle did not remember what. He said he would not remain away late. She herself was suffering from heat and oppression, she said. She carried a bottle of salts and a large fan. She would not consent to remain with Edna, for Monsieur Ratignolle was alone, and he detested above all things to be left alone.

When Étienne had fallen asleep Edna bore him into the back room, and Robert went and lifted the mosquito bar that she might lay the child comfortably in his bed. The quadroon had vanished. When they emerged from the cottage Robert bade Edna good night.

'Do you know we have been together the whole livelong day, Robert – since early this morning?' she said at parting.

'All but the hundred years when you were sleeping. Good night.'

He pressed her hand and went away in the direction of the beach. He did not join any of the others, but walked alone toward the Gulf.

Edna stayed outside, awaiting her husband's return. She had no desire to sleep or to retire; nor did she feel like going over to sit with the Ratignolles, or to join Madame Lebrun and a group whose animated voices reached her as they sat in conversation before the house. She let her mind wander back over her stay at Grand Isle, and she tried to discover wherein this summer had been different from any and every other summer of her life. She could only realize that she herself – her present self – was in some way different from the other self. That she was seeing with different eyes and making the acquaintance of new conditions in herself that colored and changed her environment, she did not yet suspect.

She wondered why Robert had gone away and left her. It did not occur to her to think he might have grown tired of being with her the livelong day. She was not tired, and she felt that he was not. She regretted that he had gone. It was so much more natural to have him stay, when he was not absolutely required to leave her.

As Edna waited for her husband she sang low a little song that Robert had sung as they crossed the bay. It began with *'Ah! Si tu savais,'*[14] and every verse ended with *'si tu savais.'*

Robert's voice was not pretentious. It was musical and true. The voice, the notes, the whole refrain haunted her memory.

14 If you knew.

XV

When Edna entered the dining room one evening a little late, as was her habit, an unusually animated conversation seemed to be going on. Several persons were talking at once, and Victor's voice was predominating, even over that of his mother. Edna had returned late from her bath, had dressed in some haste, and her face was flushed. Her head, set off by her dainty white gown, suggested a rich, rare blossom. She took her seat at table between old Monsieur Farival and Madame Ratignolle.

As she seated herself and was about to begin to eat her soup, which had been served when she entered the room, several persons informed her simultaneously that Robert was going to Mexico. She laid her spoon down and looked about her bewildered. He had been with her, reading to her all the morning, and had never even mentioned such a place as Mexico. She had not seen him during the afternoon; she had heard some one say he was at the house, upstairs with his mother. This she had thought nothing of, though she was surprised when he did not join her later in the afternoon, when she went down to the beach.

She looked across at him, where he sat beside Madame Lebrun, who presided. Edna's face was a blank picture of bewilderment, which she never thought of disguising. He lifted his eyebrows with the pretext of a smile as he returned her glance. He looked embarrassed and uneasy.

'When is he going?' she asked of everybody in general, as if Robert were not there to answer for himself.

'Tonight!' 'This very evening!' 'Did you ever!' 'What possesses him!' were some of the replies she gathered, uttered simultaneously in French and English.

'Impossible!' she exclaimed. 'How can a person start off from Grand Isle to Mexico at a moment's notice, as if he were going over to Klein's or to the wharf or down to the beach?'

'I said all along I was going to Mexico; I've been saying so for years!' cried Robert, in an excited and irritable tone, with the air of a man defending himself against a swarm of stinging insects.

Madame Lebrun knocked on the table with her knife handle.

'Please let Robert explain why he is going, and why he is going tonight,' she called out. 'Really, this table is getting to be more and more like Bedlam every day, with everybody talking at once. Sometimes – I hope God will forgive me – but positively, sometimes I wish Victor would lose the power of speech.'

Victor laughed sardonically as he thanked his mother for her holy wish, of which he failed to see the benefit to anybody, except that it might afford her a more ample opportunity and license to talk herself.

Monsieur Farival thought that Victor should have been taken out in midocean in his earliest youth and drowned. Victor thought there would be more logic in thus disposing of old people with an established claim for making themselves universally obnoxious. Madame Lebrun grew a trifle hysterical; Robert called his brother some sharp, hard names.

'There's nothing much to explain, mother,' he said, though he explained, nevertheless – looking chiefly at Edna – that he could only meet the gentleman whom he intended to join at Vera Cruz by taking such and such a steamer, which left New Orleans on such a day; that Beaudelet was going out with his lugger-load of vegetables that night, which gave him an opportunity of reaching the city and making his vessel in time.

'But when did you make up your mind to all this?' demanded Monsieur Farival.

'This afternoon,' returned Robert, with a shade of annoyance.

'At what time this afternoon?' persisted the old gentleman, with nagging determination, as if he were cross-questioning a criminal in a court of justice.

'At four o'clock this afternoon, Monsieur Farival,' Robert replied, in a high voice and with a lofty air, which reminded Edna of some gentleman on the stage.

She had forced herself to eat most of her soup,

and now she was picking the flaky bits of a *court bouillon*[15] with her fork.

The lovers were profiting by the general conversation on Mexico to speak in whispers of matters which they rightly considered were interesting to no one but themselves. The lady in black had once received a pair of prayer-beads of curious workmanship from Mexico, with very special indulgence attached to them, but she had never been able to ascertain whether the indulgence extended outside the Mexican border. Father Fochel of the Cathedral had attempted to explain it; but he had not done so to her satisfaction. And she begged that Robert would interest himself, and discover, if possible, whether she was entitled to the indulgence accompanying the remarkably curious Mexican prayer-beads.

Madame Ratignolle hoped that Robert would exercise extreme caution in dealing with the Mexicans, who, she considered, were a treacherous people, unscrupulous and revengeful. She trusted she did them no injustice in thus condemning them as a race. She had known personally but one Mexican, who made and sold excellent tamales, and whom she would have trusted implicitly, so soft-spoken was he. One day he was arrested for stabbing his wife. She never knew whether he had been hanged or not.

15 A fish stew, usually made of red snapper, tomatoes, onions, and spices.

Victor had grown hilarious, and was attempting to tell an anecdote about a Mexican girl who served chocolate one winter in a restaurant in Dauphine Street. No one would listen to him but old Monsieur Farival, who went into convulsions over the droll story.

Edna wondered if they had all gone mad, to be talking and clamoring at that rate. She herself could think of nothing to say about Mexico or the Mexicans.

'At what time do you leave?' she asked Robert.

'At ten,' he told her. 'Beaudelet wants to wait for the moon.'

'Are you all ready to go?'

'Quite ready. I shall only take a handbag, and shall pack my trunk in the city.'

He turned to answer some question put to him by his mother, and Edna, having finished her black coffee, left the table.

She went directly to her room. The little cottage was close and stuffy after leaving the outer air. But she did not mind; there appeared to be a hundred different things demanding her attention indoors. She began to set the toilet stand to rights, grumbling at the negligence of the quadroon, who was in the adjoining room putting the children to bed. She gathered together stray garments that were hanging on the backs of chairs, and put each where it belonged in closet or bureau drawer. She changed her gown for a more comfortable and commodious wrapper. She rearranged her hair, combing and brushing it with unusual energy. Then she went in and assisted the quadroon in getting the boys to bed.

They were very playful and inclined to talk – to do anything but lie quiet and go to sleep. Edna sent the quadroon away to her supper and told her she need not return. Then she sat and told the children a story. Instead of soothing it excited them, and added to their wakefulness. She left them in heated argument, speculating about the conclusion of the tale which their mother promised to finish the following night.

The little black girl came in to say that Madame Lebrun would like to have Mrs Pontellier go and sit with them over at the house till Mr Robert went away. Edna returned answer that she had already undressed, that she did not feel quite well, but perhaps she would go over to the house later. She started to dress again, and got as far advanced as to remove her *peignoir*. But changing her mind once more she resumed the *peignoir*, and went outside and sat down before her door. She was overheated and irritable, and fanned herself energetically for a while. Madame Ratignolle came down to discover what was the matter.

'All that noise and confusion at the table must have upset me,' replied Edna, 'and moreover, I hate shocks and surprises. The idea of Robert starting off in such a ridiculously sudden and dramatic way! As if it were a matter of life and death! Never saying a word about it all morning when he was with me.'

'Yes,' agreed Madame Ratignolle. 'I think it was showing us all – you especially – very little consideration. It wouldn't have surprised me in any of the others; those Lebruns are all given to heroics. But I must say I should never have expected such a thing from Robert. Are you not coming down? Come on, dear; it doesn't look friendly.'

'No,' said Edna, a little sullenly. 'I can't go to the trouble of dressing again; I don't feel like it.'

'You needn't dress; you look all right; fasten a belt around your waist. Just look at me!'

'No,' persisted Edna; 'but you go on. Madame Lebrun might be offended if we both stayed away.'

Madame Ratignolle kissed Edna goodnight, and went away, being in truth rather desirous of joining in the general and animated conversation which was still in progress concerning Mexico and the Mexicans.

Somewhat later Robert came up, carrying his handbag.

'Aren't you feeling well?' he asked.

'Oh, well enough. Are you going right away?'

He lit a match and looked at his watch. 'In twenty minutes,' he said. The sudden and brief flare of the match emphasized the darkness for a while. He sat down upon a stool which the children had left out on the porch.

'Get a chair,' said Edna.

'This will do,' he replied. He put on his soft hat and nervously took it off again, and wiping his face with his handkerchief, complained of the heat.

'Take the fan,' said Edna, offering it to him.

'Oh, no! Thank you. It does no good; you have to stop fanning sometime, and feel all the more uncomfortable afterward.'

'That's one of the ridiculous things which men always say. I have never known one to speak otherwise of fanning. How long will you be gone?'

'Forever, perhaps. I don't know. It depends upon a good many things.'

'Well, in case it shouldn't be forever, how long will it be?'

'I don't know.'

'This seems to me perfectly preposterous and uncalled for. I don't like it. I don't understand your motive for silence and mystery, never saying a word to me about it this morning.' He remained silent, not offering to defend himself. He only said, after a moment:

'Don't part from me in an ill-humor. I never knew you to be out of patience with me before.'

'I don't want to part in any ill-humor,' she said. 'But can't you understand? I've grown used to seeing you, to having you with me all the time, and your action seems unfriendly, even unkind. You don't even offer an excuse for it. Why, I was planning to be together, thinking of how pleasant it would be to see you in the city next winter.'

'So was I,' he blurted. 'Perhaps that's the – ' He stood up suddenly and held out his hand. 'Good-by, my dear Mrs Pontellier; good-by. You won't – I hope you won't completely forget me.' She clung to his hand, striving to detain him.

'Write to me when you get there, won't you, Robert?' she entreated.

'I will, thank you. Good-by.'

How unlike Robert! The merest acquaintance would have said something more emphatic than 'I will, thank you; good-by,' to such a request.

He had evidently already taken leave of the people over at the house, for he descended the steps and went to join Beaudelet, who was out there with an oar across his shoulder waiting for Robert. They walked away in the darkness. She could only hear Beaudelet's voice; Robert had apparently not even spoken a word of greeting to his companion.

Edna bit her handkerchief convulsively, striving to hold back and to hide, even from herself as she would have hidden from another, the emotion which was troubling – tearing – her. Her eyes were brimming with tears.

For the first time she recognized anew the symptoms of infatuation which she had felt incipiently as a child, as a girl in her earliest teens, and later as a young woman. The recognition did not lessen the reality, the poignancy of the revelation by any suggestion or promise of instability. The past was nothing to her; offered no lesson which she was willing to heed. The future was a mystery which she never attempted to penetrate. The present alone was significant, was hers, to torture her as it was doing then with the biting which her impassioned, newly awakened being demanded.

XVI

'Do you miss your friend greatly?' asked Mademoiselle Reisz one morning as she came creeping up behind Edna, who had just left her cottage on her way to the beach. She spent much of her time in the water since she had acquired finally the art of swimming. As their stay at Grand Isle drew near its close, she felt that she could not give too much time to a diversion which afforded her the only pleasurable moments that she knew. When Mademoiselle Reisz came and touched her upon the shoulder and spoke to her, the woman seemed to echo the thought which was ever in Edna's mind, or, better, the feeling which constantly possessed her.

Robert's going had some way taken the brightness, the color, the meaning out of everything. The conditions of her life were in no way changed, but her whole existence was dulled, like a faded garment which seems to be no longer worth wearing. She sought him everywhere – in others whom she induced to talk about him. She went up in the mornings to Madame Lebrun's room, braving the clatter of the old sewing-machine. She sat there and chatted at intervals as Robert had done. She gazed around the room at the pictures and photographs hanging upon the wall, and discovered in some corner an old family album, which she examined with the keenest interest, appealing to Madame Lebrun for enlightenment concerning the many figures and faces which she discovered between its pages.

There was a picture of Madame Lebrun with Robert as a baby, seated in her lap, a round-faced infant with a fist in his mouth. The eyes alone in the baby suggested the man. And that was he also in kilts, at the age of five, wearing long curls and holding a whip in his hand. It made Edna laugh, and she laughed, too, at the portrait in his first long trousers; while another interested her, taken when he left for college, looking thin, long-faced, with eyes full of fire, ambition and great intentions. But there was no recent picture, none which suggested the Robert who had gone away five days ago, leaving a void and wilderness behind him.

'Oh, Robert stopped having his pictures taken when he had to pay for them himself! He found wiser use for his money, he says,' explained Madame Lebrun. She had a letter from him, written before he left New Orleans. Edna wished to see the letter, and Madame Lebrun told her to look for it either on the table or the dresser, or perhaps it was on the mantelpiece.

The letter was on the bookshelf. It possessed the greatest interest and attraction for Edna; the envelope, its size and shape, the post-mark, the handwriting. She examined every detail of the outside before opening it. There were only a few lines, setting forth that he would leave the city that afternoon, that he had packed his trunk in good shape, that he was well, and sent her his love and begged to be affectionately remembered to all. There was no special message to Edna except a postscript saying that if Mrs Pontellier desired to finish the book which he had been reading to her, his mother would find it in his room, among other books there on the table. Edna experienced a pang of jealousy because he had written to his mother rather than to her.

Everyone seemed to take for granted that she missed him. Even her husband, when he came down the Saturday following Robert's departure, expressed regret that he had gone.

'How do you get on without him, Edna? he asked.

'It's very dull without him,' she admitted. Mr Pontellier had seen Robert in the city, and Edna asked him a dozen questions or more. Where had they met? On Carondelet Street, in the morning. They had gone 'in' and had a drink and a cigar together. What had they talked about? Chiefly about his prospects in Mexico, which Mr Pontellier thought were promising. How did he look? How did he seem – grave, or gay, or how? Quite cheerful, and wholly taken up with the idea of his trip, which Mr Pontellier found altogether natural in a young fellow about to seek fortune and adventure in a strange, queer country.

Edna tapped her foot impatiently, and wondered why the children persisted in playing in the sun when they might be under the trees. She went down and led them out of the sun, scolding the quadroon for not being more attentive.

It did not strike her as in the least grotesque that she should be making of Robert the object of conversation and leading her husband to speak of him. The sentiment which she entertained for Robert in no way resembled that which she felt for her husband, or had ever felt, or ever expected to feel. She had all her life long been accustomed to harbor thoughts and emotions which never voiced themselves. They had never taken the form of struggles. They belonged to her and were her own, and she entertained the conviction that she had a right to them and that they concerned no one but herself. Edna had once told Madame Ratignolle that she would never sacrifice herself for her children, or for any one. Then had followed a rather heated argument; the two women did not appear to understand each other or to be talking the same language. Edna tried to appease her friend, to explain.

'I would give up the unessential; I would give my money, I would give my life for my children; but I wouldn't give myself. I can't make it more clear; it's only something which I am beginning to comprehend, which is revealing itself to me.'

'I don't know what you would call the essential, or what you mean by the unessential,' said Madame Ratignolle, cheerfully, 'but a woman who would give her life for her children could do no more than that

– your Bible tells you so. I'm sure I couldn't do more than that.'

'Oh, yes you could!' laughed Edna.

She was not surprised at Mademoiselle Reisz's question the morning that lady, following her to the beach, tapped her on the shoulder and asked if she did not greatly miss her young friend.

'Oh, good morning. Mademoiselle; is it you? Why, of course I miss Robert. Are you going down to bathe?'

'Why should I go down to bathe at the very end of the season when I haven't been in the surf all summer,' replied the woman, disagreeably.

'I beg your pardon,' offered Edna, in some embarrassment, for she should have remembered that Mademoiselle Reisz's avoidance of the water had furnished a theme for much pleasantry. Some among them thought it was on account of her false hair, or the dread of getting the violets wet, while others attributed it to the natural aversion for water sometimes believed to accompany the artistic temperament. Mademoiselle offered Edna some chocolates in a paper bag, which she took from her pocket by way of showing that she bore no ill feeling. She habitually ate chocolates for their sustaining quality; they contained much nutriment in small compass, she said. They saved her from starvation, as Madame Lebrun's table was utterly impossible, and no one save so impertinent a woman as Madame Lebrun could think of offering such food to people and requiring them to pay for it.

'She must feel very lonely without her son,' said Edna, desiring to change the subject. 'Her favorite son, too. It must have been quite hard to let him go.'

Mademoiselle laughed maliciously.

'Her favorite son! Oh, dear! Who could have been imposing such a tale upon you? Aline Lebrun lives for Victor, and for Victor alone. She has spoiled him into the worthless creature he is. She worships him and the ground he walks on. Robert is very well in a way, to give up all the money he can earn to the family, and keep the barest pittance for himself. Favorite son, indeed! I miss the poor fellow myself, my dear. I liked to see him and to hear him about the place – the only Lebrun who is worth a pinch of salt. He comes to see me often in the city. I like to play to him. That Victor! hanging would be too good for him. It's a wonder Robert hasn't beaten him to death long ago.'

'I thought he had great patience with his brother,' offered Edna, glad to be talking about Robert, no matter what was said.

'Oh! he thrashed him well enough a year or two ago,' said Mademoiselle. 'It was about a Spanish girl, whom Victor considered that he had some sort of claim upon. He met Robert one day talking to the girl, or walking with her, or bathing with her, or carrying her basket – I don't remember what – and he became so insulting and abusive that Robert gave him a thrashing on the spot that has kept him comparatively in order for a good while. It's about time he was getting another.'

'Was her name Mariequita?' asked Edna.

'Mariequita – yes, that was it; Mariequita. I had forgotten. Oh, she's a sly one, and a bad one, that Mariequita!'

Edna looked down at Mademoiselle Reisz and wondered how she could have listened to her venom so long. For some reason she felt depressed, almost unhappy. She had not intended to go into the water; but she donned her bathing suit, and left Mademoiselle alone, seated under the shade of the children's tent. The water was growing cooler as the season advanced. Edna plunged and swam about with an abandon that thrilled and invigorated her. She remained a long time in the water, half hoping that Mademoiselle Reisz would not wait for her.

But Mademoiselle waited. She was very amiable during the walk back, and raved much over Edna's appearance in her bathing suit. She talked about music. She hoped that Edna would go to see her in the city, and wrote her address with the stub of a pencil on a piece of card which she found in her pocket.

'When do you leave?' asked Edna.

'Next Monday; and you?'

'The following week,' answered Edna, adding, 'It has been a pleasant summer, hasn't it, Mademoiselle?'

'Well,' agreed Mademoiselle Reisz, with a shrug, 'rather pleasant, if it hadn't been for the mosquitoes and the Farival twins.'

XVII

The Pontelliers possessed a very charming home on Esplanada Street in New Orleans. It was a large, double cottage, with a broad front veranda, whose round, fluted columns supported the sloping roof. The house was painted a dazzling white; the outside shutters, or jalousies, were green. In the yard, which was kept scrupulously neat, were flowers and plants of every description which flourishes in South Louisiana. Within doors the appointments were perfect after the conventional type. The softest carpets and rugs covered the floors; rich and tasteful draperies hung at doors and windows. There were paintings, selected with judgment and discrimination, upon the walls. The cut glass, the silver, the heavy damask which daily appeared upon the table were the envy of many women whose husbands were less generous than Mr Pontellier.

Mr Pontellier was very fond of walking about his house examining its various appointments and details, to see that nothing was amiss. He greatly valued his possessions, chiefly because they were his, and derived genuine pleasure from contemplating a painting, a statuette, a rare lace curtain – no matter what – after he had bought it and placed it among his household gods.

On Tuesday afternoons – Tuesday being Mrs Pontellier's reception day – there was a constant stream of callers – women who came in carriages or in the streetcars, or walked when the air was soft and distance permitted. A light-colored mulatto boy, in dress coat and bearing a diminutive silver tray for the reception of cards, admitted them. A maid, in white fluted cap, offered the callers liqueur, coffee, or chocolate, as they might desire. Mrs Pontellier, attired in a handsome reception gown, remained in the drawing room the entire afternoon receiving her visitors. Men sometimes called in the evening with their wives.

This had been the programme which Mrs Pontellier had religiously followed since her marriage, six years before. Certain evenings during the week she and her husband attended the opera or sometimes the play.

Mr Pontellier left his home in the mornings between nine and ten o'clock and rarely returned before half past six or seven in the evening – dinner being served at half-past seven.

He and his wife seated themselves at table one Tuesday evening, a few weeks after their return from Grand Isle. They were alone together. The boys were being put to bed; the patter of their bare, escaping feet could be heard occasionally, as well as the pursuing voice of the quadroon, lifted in mild protest and entreaty. Mrs Pontellier did not wear her usual Tuesday reception gown; she was in ordinary house dress. Mr Pontellier, who was observant about such things, noticed it, as he served the soup and handed it to the boy in waiting.

'Tired out, Edna? Whom did you have? Many callers?' he asked. He tasted his soup and began to season it with pepper, salt, vinegar, mustard – everything within reach.

'There were a good many,' replied Edna, who was eating her soup with evident satisfaction. 'I found their cards when I got home; I was out.'

'Out!' exclaimed her husband, with something like genuine consternation in his voice as he laid down the vinegar cruet and looked at her through his glasses. 'Why, what could have taken you out on Tuesday? What did you have to do?'

'Nothing. I simply felt like going out, and I went out.'

'Well, I hope you left some suitable excuse,' said her husband, somewhat appeased, as he added a dash of cayenne pepper to the soup.

'No, I left no excuse. I told Joe to say I was out, that was all.'

'Why, my dear, I should think you'd understand by this time that people don't do such things; we've got to observe *les convenances*[16] if we ever expect to get on and keep up with the procession. If you felt that you had to leave home this afternoon, you should have left some suitable explanation for your absence.

'This soup is really impossible; it's strange that

16 The conventions.

woman hasn't learned yet to make a decent soup. Any free lunch stand in town serves a better one. Was Mrs Belthrop here?'

'Bring the tray with the cards, Joe. I don't remember who was here.'

The boy retired and returned after a moment, bringing the tiny silver tray, which was covered with ladies' visiting cards. He handed it to Mrs Pontellier.

'Give it to Mr Pontellier,' she said.

Joe offered the tray to Mr Pontellier, and removed the soup.

Mr Pontellier scanned the names of his wife's callers, reading some of them aloud, with comments as he read.

'"The Misses Delasidas." I worked a big deal in futures for their father this morning; nice girls; it's time they were getting married. "Mrs Belthrop." I tell you what it is, Edna; you can't afford to snub Mrs Belthrop. Why, Belthrop could buy and sell us ten times over. His business is worth a good, round sum to me. You'd better write her a note. "Mrs James Highcamp." Hugh! the less you have to do with Mrs Highcamp, the better. "Madame Laforcé.' Came all the way from Carrolton, too, poor old soul. "Miss Wiggs," "Mrs Eleanor Boltons."' He pushed the cards aside.

'Mercy!' exclaimed Edna, who had been fuming. 'Why are you taking the thing so seriously and making such a fuss over it?'

'I'm not making any fuss over it. But it's just such

seeming trifles that we've got to take seriously; such things count.'

The fish was scorched. Mr Pontellier would not touch it. Edna said she did not mind a little scorched taste. The roast was in some way not to his fancy, and he did not like the manner in which the vegetables were served.

'It seems to me,' he said, 'we spend money enough in this house to procure at least one meal a day which a man could eat and retain his self-respect.'

'You used to think the cook was a treasure,' returned Edna, indifferently.

'Perhaps she was when she first came; but cooks are only human. They need looking after, like any other class of persons that you employ. Suppose I didn't look after the clerks in my office, just let them run things their own way; they'd soon make a nice mess of me and my business.'

'Where are you going?' asked Edna, seeing that her husband arose from table without having eaten a morsel except a taste of the highly-seasoned soup.

'I'm going to get my dinner at the club. Good night.' He went into the hall, took his hat and stick from the stand, and left the house.

She was somewhat familiar with such scenes. They had often made her very unhappy. On a few previous occasions she had been completely deprived of any desire to finish her dinner. Sometimes she had gone into the kitchen to adminster a tardy rebuke to the cook. Once she went to her room and studied the cookbook during an entire evening, finally writing out a menu for the week, which left her harassed with a feeling that, after all, she had accomplished no good that was worth the name.

But that evening Edna finished her dinner alone, with forced deliberation. Her face was flushed and her eyes flamed with some inward fire that lighted them. After finishing her dinner she went to her room, having instructed the boy to tell any other callers that she was indisposed.

It was a large, beautiful room, rich and pictur-esque in the soft, dim light which the maid had turned low. She went and stood at an open window and looked out upon the deep tangle of the garden below. All the mystery and witchery of the night seemed to have gathered there amid the perfumes and the dusky and tortuous outlines of flowers and foliage. She was seeking herself and finding herself in just such sweet, half darkness which met her moods. But the voices were not soothing that came to her from the darkness and the sky above and the stars. They jeered and sounded mournful notes without promise, devoid even of hope. She turned back into the room and began to walk to and fro down its whole length, without stopping, without resting. She carried in her hands a thin handker-chief, which she tore into ribbons, rolled into a ball, and flung from her. Once she stopped, and taking off her wedding ring, flung it upon the carpet. When she saw it lying there, she stamped her heel upon it, striving to crush it. But her small boot heel did not make an indenture, not a mark upon the little glittering circlet.

In a sweeping passion she seized a glass vase from the table and flung it upon the tiles of the hearth. She wanted to destroy something. The crash and clatter were what she wanted to hear.

A maid, alarmed at the din of breaking glass, entered the room to discover what was the matter.

'A vase fell upon the hearth,' said Edna. 'Never mind; leave it till morning.'

'Oh! you might get some of the glass in your feet, ma'am,' insisted the young woman, picking up bits of the broken vase that were scattered upon the carpet. 'And here's your ring, ma'am, under the chair.'

Edna held out her hand, and taking the ring, slipped it upon her finger.

XVIII

The following morning, Mr Pontellier, upon leaving for his office, asked Edna if she would not meet him in town in order to look at some new fixtures for the library.

'I hardly think we need new fixtures, Léonce. Don't let us get anything new; you are too extravagant. I don't believe you ever think of saving or putting by.'

'The way to become rich is to make money, my dear Edna, not to save it,' he said. He regretted that she did not feel inclined to go with him and select new fixtures. He kissed her good-by, and told her she was not looking well and must take care of herself. She was unusually pale and very quiet.

She stood on the front veranda as he quitted the house, and absently picked a few sprays of jessamine that grew upon a trellis near by. She inhaled the odor of the blossoms and thrust them into the bosom of her white morning gown. The boys were dragging along the banquette a small 'express wagon', which they had filled with blocks and sticks. The quadroon was following them with little quick steps, having assumed a fictitious animation and alacrity for the occasion. A fruit vender was crying his wares in the street.

Edna looked straight before her with a self-absorbed expression upon her face. She felt no interest in anything about her. The street, the children, the fruit vender, the flowers growing there under her eyes, were all part and parcel of an alien world which had suddenly become antagonistic.

She went back into the house. She had thought of speaking to the cook concerning her blunders of the previous night; but Mr Pontellier had saved her that disagreeable mission, for which she was so poorly fitted. Mr Pontellier's arguments were usually convincing with those whom he employed. He left home feeling quite sure that he and Edna would sit down that evening, and possibly a few subsequent evenings, to a dinner deserving of the name.

Edna spent an hour or two in looking over some of her old sketches. She could see their shortcomings and defects, which were glaring in her eyes. She tried to work a little, but found she was not in the humor. Finally she gathered together a few of the sketches – those which she considered the least discreditable; and she carried them with her when, a little later, she dressed and left the house. She looked handsome and distinguished in her street gown. The tan of the seashore had left her face, and her forehead was smooth, white, and polished beneath her heavy, yellow-brown hair. There were a few freckles on her face, and a small, dark mole near the under lip and one on the temple, half-hidden in her hair.

As Edna walked along the street she was thinking of Robert. She was still under the spell of her infatuation. She had tried to forget him, realizing the inutility of remembering. But the thought of him was like an obsession, ever pressing itself upon her. It was not that she dwelt upon details of their acquaintance, or recalled in any special or peculiar way his personality; it was his being, his existence, which dominated her thought, fading sometimes as if it would melt into the mist of the forgotten, reviving again with an intensity which filled her with an incomprehensible longing.

Edna was on her way to Madame Ratignolle's. Their intimacy begun at Grand Isle, had not declined, and they had seen each other with some frequency since their return to the city. The Ratignolles lived at no great distance from Edna's home, on the corner of a side street, where Monsieur Ratignolle owned and conducted a drug store which enjoyed a steady and prosperous trade. His father had been in the business before him, and Monsieur Ratignolle stood well in the community and bore an enviable reputation for integrity and clearheadedness. His family lived in commodious apartments over the store, having an entrance on the side within the *porte cochère.* There was something which Edna thought very French, very foreign, about their whole manner of living. In the large and pleasant salon which extended across the width of the house, the Ratignolles entertained their friends once a fortnight with a *soirée musicale,*[17] sometimes diversified

17 An evening of musical entertainment.

by card-playing. There was a friend who played upon the 'cello. One brought his flute and another his violin, while there were some who sang and a number who performed upon the piano with various degrees of taste and agility. The Ratignolles' *soirées musicales* were widely known, and it was considered a privilege to be invited to them.

Edna found her friend engaged in assorting the clothes which had returned that morning from the laundry. She at once abandoned her occupation upon seeing Edna, who had been ushered without ceremony into her presence.

'Cité can do it as well as I; it is really her business,' she explained to Edna, who apologized for interrupting her. And she summoned a young black woman, whom she instructed, in French, to be very careful in checking off the list which she handed her. She told her to notice particularly if a fine linen handkerchief of Monsieur Ratignolle's, which was missing last week, had been returned; and to be sure to set to one side such pieces as required mending and darning.

Then placing an arm around Edna's waist, she led her to the front of the house, to the salon, where it was cool and sweet with the odor of great roses that stood upon the hearth in jars.

Madame Ratignolle looked more beautiful than ever there at home, in a *negligée* which left her arms almost wholly bare and exposed the rich, melting curves of her white throat.

'Perhaps I shall be able to paint your picture

some day,' said Edna with a smile when they were seated. She produced the roll of sketches and started to unfold them. 'I believe I ought to work again. I feel as if I wanted to be doing something. What do you think of them? Do you think it worth while to take it up again and study some more? I might study for a while with Laidpore.'

She knew that Madame Ratignolle's opinion in such a matter would be next to valueless, that she herself had not alone decided, but determined; but she sought the words of praise and encouragement that would help her to put heart into her venture.

'Your talent is immense, dear!'

'Nonsense!' protested Edna, well pleased.

'Immense, I tell you,' persisted Madame Ratignolle, surveying the sketches one by one, at close range, then holding them at arm's length, narrowing her eyes, and dropping her head on one side. 'Surely, this Bavarian peasant is worthy of framing; and this basket of apples! never have I seen anything more lifelike. One might almost be tempted to reach out a hand and take one.'

Edna could not control a feeling which bordered upon complacency at her friend's praise, even realizing, as she did, its true worth. She retained a few of the sketches, and gave all the rest to Madame Ratignolle, who appreciated the gift far beyond its value and proudly exhibited the pictures to her husband when he came up from the store a little later for his midday dinner.

Mr Ratignolle was one of those men who are

called the salt of the earth. His cheerfulness was unbounded, and it was matched by his goodness of heart, his broad charity, and common sense. He and his wife spoke English with an accent which was only discernible through its un-English emphasis and a certain carefulness and deliberation. Edna's husband spoke English with no accent whatever. The Ratignolles understood each other perfectly. If ever the fusion of two human beings into one has been accomplished on this sphere it was surely in their union.

As Edna seated herself at table with them she thought, 'Better a dinner of herbs,' though it did not take her long to discover that was no dinner of herbs, but a delicious repast, simple, choice, and in every way satisfying.

Monsieur Ratignolle was delighted to see her, though he found her looking not so well as at Grand Isle, and he advised a tonic. He talked a good deal on various topics, a little politics, some city news and neighbourhood gossip. He spoke with an animation and earnestness that gave an exaggerated importance to every syllable he uttered. His wife was keenly interested in everything he said, laying down her fork the better to listen, chiming in, taking the words out of his mouth.

Edna felt depressed rather than soothed after leaving them. The little glimpse of domestic harmony which had been offered her, gave her no regret, no longing. It was not a condition of life which fitted her, and she could see in it but an appalling and hopeless ennui. She was moved by a kind of commiseration for Madame Ratignolle – a pity for that colorless existence which never uplifted its possessor beyond the region of blind contentment, in which no moment of anguish ever visited her soul, in which she would never have the taste of life's delirium. Edna vaguely wondered what she meant by 'life's delirium.' It had crossed her thought like some unsought, extraneous impression.

XIX

Edna could not help but think that it was very foolish, very childish, to have stamped upon her wedding ring and smashed the crystal vase upon the tiles. She was visited by no more outbursts, moving her to such futile expedients. She began to do as she liked and to feel as she liked. She completely abandoned her Tuesdays at home, and did not return the visits of those who had called upon her. She made no ineffectual efforts to conduct her household *en bonne ménagère,* going and coming as it suited her fancy, and, so far as she was able, lending herself to any passing caprice.

Mr Pontellier had been a rather courteous husband so long as he met a certain tacit submissiveness in his wife. But her new and unexpected line of conduct completely bewildered him. It shocked him. Then her absolute disregard for her duties as a wife angered him. When Mr Pontellier became rude, Edna grew insolent. She had resolved never to take another step backward.

'It seems to me the utmost folly for a woman at the head of a household, and the mother of children, to spend in an atelier days which would be better employed contriving for the comfort of her family.'

'I feel like painting,' answered Edna. 'Perhaps I shan't always feel like it.'

'Then in God's name paint! but don't let the family go to the devil. There's Madame Ratignolle; because she keeps up her music, she doesn't let everything go to chaos. And she's more of a musician than you are a painter.'

'She isn't a musician, and I'm not a painter. It isn't on account of painting that I let things go.'

'On account of what then?'

'Oh! I don't know. Let me alone; you bother me.'

It sometimes entered Mr Pontellier's mind to wonder if his wife were not growing a little unbalanced mentally. He could see plainly that she was not herself. That is, he could not see that she was becoming herself and daily casting aside that fictitious self which we assume like a garment with which to appear before the world.

Her husband let her alone as she requested, and went away to his office. Edna went up to her atelier – a bright room in the top of the house. She was working with great energy and interest, without accomplishing anything, however, which satisfied her even in the smallest degree. For a time she had the whole household enrolled in the service of art. The boys posed for her. They thought it amusing at first, but the occupation soon lost its attractiveness when they discovered that it was not a game arranged especially for their entertainment. The quadroon sat for hours before Edna's palette, patient as a savage, while the housemaid took charge of the children, and the drawing room went undusted. But the housemaid, too, served her term as model, when Edna perceived that the young woman's back and shoulders were molded on classic lines, and that her hair, loosened from its confining cap, became an inspiration. While Edna worked she sometimes sang low the little air, *'Ah! sit tu savais!'*

It moved her with recollections. She could hear again the ripple of the water, the flapping sail. She could see the glint of the moon upon the bay, and could feel the soft, gusty beating of the hot south wind. A subtle current of desire passed through her body, weakening her hold upon the brushes and making her eyes burn.

There were days when she was very happy without knowing why. She was happy to be alive and breathing, when her whole being seemed to be one with the sunlight, the color, the odors, the luxuriant warmth of some perfect Southern day. She liked then to wander alone into strange and unfamiliar places. She discovered many a sunny, sleepy corner, fashioned to dream in. And she found it good to dream and to be alone and unmolested.

There were days when she was unhappy, she did not know why – when it did not seem worth while to be glad or sorry, to be alive or dead, when life appeared to her like a grotesque pandemonium and humanity like worms struggling blindly toward inevitable annihilation. She could not work on such a day, nor weave fancies to stir her pulses and warm her blood.

XX

It was during such a mood that Edna hunted up Mademoiselle Reisz. She had not forgotten the rather disagreeable impression left upon her by their last interview; but she nevertheless felt a desire to see her – above all, to listen while she played upon the piano. Quite early in the afternoon she started upon her quest for the pianist. Unfortunately she had mislaid or lost Mademoiselle Reisz's card, and looking up her address in the city directory, she found that the woman lived in Bienville Street, some distance away. The directory which fell into her hands was a year or more old, however, and upon reaching the number indicated, Edna discovered that the house was occupied by a respectable family of mulattoes who had *chambres garnies*[18] to let. They had been living there for six months, and knew absolutely nothing of a Mademoiselle Reisz. In fact, they knew nothing of any of their neighbors; their lodgers were all people of the highest distinction, they assured Edna. She did not linger to discuss class distinctions with Madame Pouponne, but hastened to a neighboring grocery

18 Furnished rooms.

store, feeling sure that Mademoiselle would have left her address with the proprietor.

He knew Mademoiselle Reisz a good deal better than he wanted to know her, he informed his questioner. In truth, he did not want to know her at all, or anything concerning her – the most disagreeable and unpopular woman who ever lived in Bienville Street. He thanked heaven she had left the neighborhood, and was equally thankful that he did not know where she had gone.

Edna's desire to see Mademoiselle Reisz had increased tenfold since these unlooked-for obstacles had arisen to thwart it. She was wondering who could give her the information she sought, when it suddenly occurred to her that Madame Lebrun would be the one most likely to do so. She knew it was useless to ask Madame Ratignolle, who was on the most distant terms with the musician, and preferred to know nothing concerning her. She had once been almost as emphatic in expressing herself upon the subject as the corner grocer.

Edna knew that Madame Lebrun had returned to the city, for it was the middle of November. And she also knew where the Lebruns lived, on Chartres Street.

Their home from the outside looked like a prison, with iron bars before the door and lower windows. The iron bars were a relic of the old *régime,* and no one had ever thought of dislodging them. At the side was a high fence enclosing the garden. A gate or door opening upon the street was locked. Edna rang the bell at this side garden gate, and stood upon the banquette, waiting to be admitted.

It was Victor who opened the gate for her. A black woman, wiping her hands upon her apron, was close at his heels. Before she saw them Edna could hear them in altercation, the woman – plainly an anomaly – claiming the right to be allowed to perform her duties, one of which was to answer the bell.

Victor was surprised and delighted to see Mrs Pontellier, and he made no attempt to conceal either his astonishment or his delight. He was a dark-browed, good-looking youngster of nineteen, greatly resembling his mother, but with ten times her impetuosity. He instructed the black woman to go at once and inform Madame Lebrun that Mrs Pontellier desired to see her. The woman grumbled a refusal to do part of her duty when she had not been permitted to do it all, and started back to her interrupted task of weeding the garden. Whereupon Victor administered a rebuke in the form of a volley of abuse, which, owing to its rapidity and incoherence, was all but incomprehensible to Edna. Whatever it was, the rebuke was convincing, for the woman dropped her hoe and went mumbling into the house.

Edna did not wish to enter. It was very pleasant there on the side porch, where there were chairs, a wicker lounge, and a small table. She seated herself, for she was tired from her long tramp; and she began to rock gently and smooth out the folds of her silk parasol. Victor drew up his chair beside her. He at once explained that the black woman's offensive conduct was all due to imperfect training, as he was not there to take her in hand. He had only come up from the island the morning before, and expected to return next day. He stayed all winter at the island; he lived there, and kept the place in order and got things ready for the summer visitors.

But a man needed occasional relaxation, he informed Mrs Pontellier, and every now and again he drummed up a pretext to bring him to the city. My! but he had had a time of it the evening before! He wouldn't want his mother to know, and he began to talk in a whisper. He was scintillant with recollections. Of course, he couldn't think of telling Mrs Pontellier all about it, she being a woman and not comprehending such things. But it all began with a girl peeping and smiling at him through the shutters as he passed by. Oh! but she was a beauty! certainly he smiled back and went up and talked to her. Mrs Pontellier did not know him if she supposed he was one to let an opportunity like that escape him. Despite herself, the youngster amused her. She must have betrayed in her look some degree of interest or entertainment. The boy grew more daring, and Mrs Pontellier might have found herself, in a little while, listening to a highly colored story but for the timely appearance of Madame Lebrun.

That lady was still clad in white, according to her custom of the summer. Her eyes beamed an effusive welcome. Would not Mrs Pontellier go inside? Would she partake of some refreshment? Why had she not been there before? How was that dear Mr Pontellier and how were those sweet children? Had Mrs Pontellier ever known such a warm November?

Victor went and reclined on the wicker lounge behind his mother's chair, where he commanded a view of Edna's face. He had taken her parasol from her hands while he spoke to her, and he now lifted it and twirled it above him as he lay on his back. When Madame Lebrun complained that it was *so* dull coming back to the city; that she saw *so* few people now; that even Victor, when he came up from the island for a day or two, had *so* much to occupy him and engage his time; then it was that the youth went into contortions on the lounge and winked mischievously at Edna. She somehow felt like a confederate in crime, and tried to look severe and disapproving.

There had been but two letters from Robert, with little in them, they told her. Victor said it was really not worth while to go inside for the letters, when his mother entreated him to go in search of them. He remembered the contents, which in truth he rattled off very glibly when put to the test.

One letter was written from Vera Cruz and the other from the City of Mexico. He had met Montel, who was doing everything toward his advancement. So far, the financial situation was no improvement over the one he had left in New Orleans, but of course the prospects were vastly better. He wrote of the City of Mexico, the buildings, the people and their habits, the conditions of life which he found there. He sent his love to the family. He enclosed a check to his mother, and hoped she would affectionately remember him to all his friends. That was about the substance of the two letters. Edna felt that if there had been a message for her, she would have received it. The despondent frame of mind in which she had left home began again to overtake her, and she remembered that she wished to find Mademoiselle Reisz.

Madame Lebrun knew where Mademoiselle Reisz lived. She gave Edna the address, regretting that she would not consent to stay and spend the remainder of the afternoon, and pay a visit to Mademoiselle Reisz some other day. The afternoon was already well advanced.

Victor escorted her out upon the banquette, lifted her parasol, and held it over her while he walked to the car with her. He entreated her to bear in mind that the disclosures of the afternoon were strictly confidential. She laughed and bantered him a little, remembering too late that she should have been dignified and reserved.

'How handsome Mrs Pontellier looked!' said Madame Lebrun to her son.

'Ravishing!' he admitted. 'The city atmosphere has improved her. Some way she doesn't seem like the same woman.'

XXI

Some people contended that the reason Mademoiselle Reisz always chose apartments up under the roof was to discourage the approach of beggars, peddlars and callers. There were plenty of windows in her little front room. They were for the most part dingy, but as they were nearly always open it did not make so much difference. They often admitted into the room a good deal of smoke and soot; but at the same time all the light and air that there was came through them. From her windows could be seen the crescent of the river, the masts of ships and the big chimneys of the Mississippi steamers. A magnificent piano crowded the apartment. In the next room she slept, and in the third and last she harbored a gasoline stove on which she cooked her meals when disclined to descend to the neighboring restaurant. It was there also that she ate, keeping her belongings in a rare old buffet, dingy and battered from a hundred years of use.

When Edna knocked at Mademoiselle Reisz's front room door and entered, she discovered that person standing beside the window, engaged in mending or patching an old prunella gaiter. The little musician laughed all over when she saw Edna. Her laugh consisted of a contortion of the face and all the muscles of the body. She seemed strikingly homely, standing there in the afternoon light. She still wore the shabby lace and the artificial bunch of violets on the side of her head.

'So you remembered me at last,' said Mademoiselle. 'I had said to myself, "Ah, bah! she will never come."'

'Did you want me to come?' asked Edna with a smile.

'I had not thought much about it,' answered Mademoiselle. The two had seated themselves on a little bumpy sofa which stood against the wall. 'I am glad, however, that you came. I have the water boiling back there, and was just about to make some coffee. You will drink a cup with me. And how is *la belle dame?* Always handsome! always healthy! always contented!' She took Edna's hand between her strong wiry fingers, holding it loosely without warmth, and executing a sort of double theme upon the back and palm.

'Yes,' she went on; 'I sometimes thought: "She will never come. She promised as those women in society always do, without meaning it. She will not come. For I really don't believe you like me, Mrs Pontellier."'

'I don't know whether I like you or not,' replied Edna, gazing down at the little woman with a quizzical look.

The candor of Mrs Pontellier's admission greatly pleased Mademoiselle Reisz. She expressed her gratification by repairing forthwith to the region of the gasoline stove and rewarding her guest with the promised cup of coffee. The coffee and the biscuit accompanying it proved very acceptable to Edna, who had declined refreshment at Madame Lebrun's and was now beginning to feel hungry. Mademoiselle set the tray which she brought in upon a small table near at hand, and seated herself once again on the lumpy sofa.

'I have had a letter from your friend,' she remarked, as she poured a little cream into Edna's cup and handed it to her.

'My friend?'

'Yes, your friend Robert. He wrote to me from the City of Mexico.'

'Wrote to *you?*' repeated Edna in amazement, stirring her coffee absently.

'Yes, to me. Why not? Don't stir all the warmth out of your coffee; drink it. Though the letter might as well have been sent to you; it was nothing but Mrs Pontellier from beginning to end.'

'Let me see it,' requested the young woman, entreatingly.

'No; a letter concerns no one but the person who writes it and the one to whom it is written.'

'Haven't you just said it concerned me from beginning to end?'

'It was written about you, not to you. "Have you seen Mrs Pontellier? How is she looking?" he asks. "As Mrs Pontellier says," or "as Mrs Pontellier once said." "If Mrs Pontellier should call upon you, play for her that Impromptu of Chopin's, my favorite. I heard it here a day or two ago, but not as you play it. I should like to know how it affects her," and so on, as if he supposed we were constantly in each other's society.'

'Let me see the letter.'

'Oh, no.'

'Have you answered it?'

'No.'

'Let me see the letter.'

'No, and again, no.'

'Then play the Impromptu for me.'

'It is growing late; what time do you have to be home?'

'Time doesn't concern me. Your question seems a little rude. Play the Impromptu.'

'But you have told me nothing of yourself. What are you doing?'

'Painting!' laughed Edna. 'I am becoming an artist. Think of it!'

'Ah! an artist! You have pretensions, Madame.'

'Why pretensions? Do you think I could not become an artist?'

'I do not know you well enough to say. I do not know your talent or your temperament. To be an artist includes much; one must possess many gifts – absolute gifts – which have not been acquired by one's own effort. And, moreover, to succeed, the artist must possess the courageous soul.'

'What do you mean by the courageous soul?'

'Courageous, *ma foi!* The brave soul. The soul that dares and defies.'

'Show me the letter and play for me the Impromptu. You see that I have persistence. Does that quality count for anything in art?'

'It counts with a foolish old woman whom you have captivated,' replied Mademoiselle, with her wriggling laugh.

The letter was right there at hand in the drawer of the little table upon which Edna had just placed her coffee cup. Mademoiselle opened the drawer and drew forth the letter, the topmost one. She placed it in Edna's hands, and without further comment arose and went to the piano.

Mademoiselle played a soft interlude. It was an improvisation. She sat low at the instrument, and the lines of her body settled into ungraceful curves and angles that gave it an appearance of deformity. Gradually and imperceptibly the interlude melted into the soft opening minor chords of the Chopin Impromptu.

Edna did not know when the Impromptu began or ended. She sat in the sofa corner reading Robert's letter by the fading light. Mademoiselle had glided from the Chopin into the quivering love notes of Isolde's song, and back again to the Impromptu with its soulful and poignant longing.

The shadows deepened in the little room. The music grew strange and fantastic – turbulent, insistent, plaintive and soft with entreaty. The shadows grew deeper. The music filled the room. It floated out upon the night, over the housetops, the crescent of the river, losing itself in the silence of the upper air.

Edna was sobbing, just as she had wept one midnight at Grand Isle when strange, new voices awoke in her. She arose in some agitation to take her departure. 'May I come again, Mademoiselle?' she asked at the threshold.

'Come whenever you feel like it. Be careful; the stairs and landing are dark; don't stumble.'

Mademoiselle reentered and lit a candle. Robert's letter was on the floor. She stooped and picked it up. It was crumpled and damp with tears. Mademoiselle smoothed the letter out, restored it to the envelope, and replaced it in the table drawer.

XXII

One morning on his way into town Mr Pontellier stopped at the house of his old friend and family physician, Doctor Mandelet. The Doctor was a semiretired physician, resting, as the saying is, upon his laurels. He bore a reputation for wisdom rather than skill – leaving the active practice of medicine to his assistants and younger contemporaries – and was much sought for in matters of consultation. A few families, united to him by bonds of friendship, he still attended when they required the services of a physician. The Pontelliers were among these.

Mr Pontellier found the Doctor reading at the open window of his study. His house stood rather far back from the street, in the center of a delightful garden, so that it was quiet and peaceful at the old gentleman's study window. He was a great reader. He stared up disapprovingly over his eyeglasses as Mr Pontellier entered, wondering who had the temerity to disturb him at that hour of the morning.

'Ah, Pontellier! Not sick, I hope. Come and have a seat. What news do you bring this morning?' He was quite portly, with a profusion of gray hair, and small blue eyes which age had robbed of much of their brightness but none of their penetration.

'Oh! I'm never sick, Doctor. You know that I

come of tough fiber – of that old Creole race of Pontelliers that dry up and finally blow away. I came to consult – no, not precisely to consult – to talk to you about Edna. I don't know what ails her.'

'Madame Pontellier not well?' marveled the Doctor. 'Why, I saw her – I think it was a week ago – walking along Canal Street, the picture of health, it seemed to me.'

'Yes, yes; she seems quite well,' said Mr Pontellier, leaning forward and whirling his stick between his two hands; 'but she doesn't act well. She's odd, she's not like herself. I can't make her out, and I thought perhaps you'd help me.'

'How does she act?' inquired the doctor.

'Well it isn't easy to explain,' said Mr Pontellier, throwing himself back in his chair. 'She lets the housekeeping go to the dickens.'

'Well, well; women are not all alike, my dear Pontellier. We've got to consider – '

'I know that; I told you I couldn't explain. Her whole attitude – toward me and everybody and everything – has changed. You know I have a quick temper, but I don't want to quarrel or be rude to a woman, especially my wife; yet I'm driven to it, and feel like ten thousand devils after I've made a fool of myself. She's making it devilishly uncomfortable for me,' he went on nervously. 'She's got some sort of notion in her head concerning the eternal rights of women; and – you understand – we meet in the morning at the breakfast table.'

The old gentleman lifted his shaggy eyebrows,

protruded his thick nether lip, and tapped the arms of his chair with his cushioned fingertips.

'What have you been doing to her, Pontellier?'

'Doing! *Parbleu!*'

'Has she,' asked the Doctor, with a smile, 'has she been associating of late with a circle of pseudo-intellectual women – superspiritual superior beings? My wife has been telling me about them.'

'That's the trouble,' broke in Mr Pontellier, 'she hasn't been associating with any one. She has abandoned her Tuesdays at home, has thrown over all her acquaintances, and goes tramping about by herself, moping in the street cars, getting in after dark. I tell you she's peculiar. I don't like it; I feel a little worried over it.'

This was a new aspect for the Doctor. 'Nothing hereditary?' he asked, seriously. 'Nothing peculiar about her family antecedents, is there?'

'Oh, no, indeed! She comes of sound old Presbyterian Kentucky stock. The old gentleman, her father, I have heard, used to atone for his weekday sins with his Sunday devotions. I know for a fact, that his race horses literally ran away with the prettiest bit of Kentucky farming land I ever laid eyes upon. Margaret – you know Margaret – she has all the Presbyterianism undiluted. And the youngest is something of a vixen. By the way, she gets married in a couple of weeks from now.'

'Send your wife up to the wedding,' exclaimed the Doctor, foreseeing a happy solution. 'Let her stay among her own people for a while; it will do her good.'

'That's what I want her to do. She won't go to the marriage. She says a wedding is one of the most lamentable spectacles on earth. Nice thing for a woman to say to her husband!' exclaimed Mr Pontellier, fuming anew at the recollection.

'Pontellier,' said the Doctor, after a moment's reflection, 'let your wife alone for a while. Don't bother her, and don't let her bother you. Woman, my dear friend, is a very peculiar and delicate organism – a sensitive and highly organized woman, such as I know Mrs Pontellier to be, is especially peculiar. It would require an inspired psychologist to deal successfully with them. And when ordinary fellows like you and me attempt to cope with their idiosyncrasies the result is bungling. Most women are moody and whimsical. This is some passing whim of your wife, due to some cause or causes which you and I needn't try to fathom. But it will pass happily over, especially if you let her alone. Send her around to see me.'

'Oh! I couldn't do that; there'd be no reason for it,' objected Mr Pontellier.

'Then I'll go around and see her,' said the Doctor. 'I'll drop in to dinner some evening *en bon ami*.'[19]

'Do! by all means,' urged Mr Pontellier. 'What

19 Informally; as a good friend.

evening will you come? Say Thursday. Will you come Thursday?' he asked, rising to take his leave.

'Very well; Thursday. My wife may possibly have some engagement for me Thursday. In case she has, I shall let you know. Otherwise, you may expect me.'

Mr Pontellier turned before leaving to say:

'I am going to New York on business very soon. I have a big scheme on hand, and want to be on the field proper to pull the ropes and handle the ribbons. We'll let you in on the inside if you say so, Doctor,' he laughed.

'No, I thank you, my dear sir,' returned the Doctor. 'I leave such ventures to you younger men with the fever of life still in your blood.'

'What I wanted to say,' continued Mr Pontellier, with his hand on the knob; 'I may have to be absent a good while. Would you advise me to take Edna along?'

'By all means, if she wishes to go. If not, leave her here. Don't contradict her. The mood will pass, I assure you. It may take a month, two, three months – possibly longer, but it will pass; have patience.'

'Well good-by, *à jeudi*,'[20] said Mr Pontellier, as he let himself out.

The Doctor would have liked during the course of conversation to ask, 'Is there any man in the case?' but he knew his Creole too well to make such a blunder as that.

He did not resume his book immediately, but sat for a while meditatively looking out into the garden.

20 Until Thursday.

XXIII

Edna's father was in the city, and had been with them several days. She was not very warmly or deeply attached to him, but they had certain tastes in common, and when together they were companionable. His coming was in the nature of a welcome disturbance; it seemed to furnish a new direction for her emotions.

He had come to purchase a wedding gift for his daughter, Janet, and an outfit for himself in which he might make a creditable appearance at her marriage. Mr Pontellier had selected the bridal gift, as everyone immediately connected with him always deferred to his taste in such matters. And his suggestions on the question of dress – which too often assumes the nature of a problem – were of inestimable value to his father-in-law. But for the past few days the old gentleman had been upon Edna's hands, and in his society she was becoming acquainted with a new set of sensations. He had been a colonel in the Confederate army, and still maintained, with the title, the military bearing which had always accompanied it. His hair and mustache were white and silky, emphasizing the rugged bronze of his face. He was tall and thin, and wore his coats padded, which gave a fictitious breadth and depth to his shoulders and chest. Edna and her father looked very distinguished together, and excited a good deal of notice during their perambulations. Upon his arrival she began by introducing him to her atelier and making a sketch of him. He took the whole matter very seriously. If her talent had been tenfold greater than it was, it would not have surprised him, convinced as he was that he had bequeathed to all of his daughters the germs of a masterful capability, which only depended upon their own efforts to be directed toward successful achievement.

Before her pencil he sat rigid and unflinching, as he had faced the cannon's mouth in days gone by. He resented the intrusion of the children, who gaped with wondering eyes at him, sitting so stiff up there in their mother's bright atelier. When they drew near he motioned them away with an expressive action of the foot, loath to disturb the fixed lines of his countenance, his arms, or his rigid shoulders.

Edna, anxious to entertain him, invited Mademoiselle Reisz to meet him, having promised him a treat in her piano playing; but Mademoiselle declined the invitation. So together they attended a *soiree musicale* at the Ratignolles'. Monsieur and Madame Ratignolle made much of the Colonel, installing him as the guest of honor and engaging him at once to dine with them the following Sunday, or any day which he might select. Madame coquetted with him in the most captivating and naïve manner, with eyes, gestures, and a profusion of compliments, till the Colonel's old head felt thirty years younger on his padded shoulders. Edna marvelled, not comprehending. She herself was almost devoid of coquetry.

There were one or two men whom she observed at the *soirée musicale;* but she would never have felt moved to any kittenish display to attract their notice – to any feline or feminine wiles to express herself toward them. Their personality attracted her in an agreeable way. Her fancy selected them, and she was glad when a lull in the music gave them an opportunity to meet her and talk with her. Often on the street the glance of strange eyes had lingered in her memory, and sometimes had disturbed her.

Mr Pontellier did not attend these *soirées musicales.* He considered them *bourgeois,* and found more diversion at the club. To Madame Ratignolle he said the music dispensed at her *soirées* was too 'heavy,' too far beyond his untrained comprehension. His excuse flattered her. But she disapproved of Mr Pontellier's club, and she was frank enough to tell Edna so.

'It's a pity Mr Pontellier doesn't stay home more in the evenings. I think you would be more – well, if you don't mind my saying it – more united, if he did.'

'Oh! dear no!' said Edna, with a blank look in her eyes. 'What should I do if he stayed home? We wouldn't have anything to say to each other.'

She had not much of anything to say to her

father, for that matter; but he did not antagonize her. She discovered that he interested her, though she realized that he might not interest her long; and for the first time in her life she felt as if she were thoroughly acquainted with him. He kept her busy serving him and ministering to his wants. It amused her to do so. She would not permit a servant or one of the children to do anything for him which she might do herself. Her husband noticed, and thought it was the expression of a deep filial attachment which he had never suspected.

The Colonel drank numerous 'toddies' during the course of the day, which left him, however, unperturbed. He was an expert at concocting strong drinks. He had even invented some, to which he had given fantastic names, and for whose manufacture he required diverse ingredients that it devolved upon Edna to procure for him.

When Doctor Mandelet dined with the Pontelliers on Thursday he could discern in Mrs Pontellier no trace of that morbid condition which her husband had reported to him. She was excited and in a manner radiant. She and her father had been to the race course, and their thoughts when they seated themselves at table were still occupied with the events of the afternoon, and their talk was still of the track. The Doctor had not kept pace with turf affairs. He had certain recollections of racing in what he called 'the good old times' when the Lecompte stables flourished, and he drew upon this fund of memories so that he might not be left out and seem wholly devoid of the modern spirit. But he failed to impose upon the Colonel, and was even far from impressing him with this trumped-up knowledge of bygone days. Edna had staked her father on his last venture, with the most gratifying results to both of them. Besides, they had met some very charming people, according to the Colonel's impressions. Mrs Mortimer Merriman and Mrs James Highcamp, who were there with Alcée Arobin, had joined them and had enlivened the hours in a fashion that warmed him to think of.

Mr Pontellier himself had no particular leaning toward horse racing, and was even rather inclined to discourage it as a pastime, especially when he considered the fate of that bluegrass farm in Kentucky. He endeavoured, in a general way, to express a particular disapproval, and only succeeded in arousing the ire and opposition of his father-in-law. A pretty dispute followed, in which Edna warmly espoused her father's cause and the Doctor remained neutral.

He observed his hostess attentively from under his shaggy brows, and noted a subtle change which had transformed her from the listless woman he had known into a being who, for the moment, seemed palpitant with the forces of life. Her speech was warm and energetic. There was no repression in her glance or gesture. She reminded him of some beautiful, sleek animal waking up in the sun.

The dinner was excellent. The claret was warm and the champagne was cold, and under their beneficent influence the threatened unpleasantness melted and vanished with the fumes of the wine.

Mr Pontellier warmed up and grew reminiscent. He told some amusing plantation experiences, recollections of old Iberville and his youth, when he hunted 'possum in company with some friendly darky; thrashed the pecan trees, shot the grosbec, and roamed the woods and fields in mischievous idleness.

The Colonel, with little sense of humor and of the fitness of things, related a somber episode of those dark and bitter days, in which he had acted a conspicuous part and always formed a central figure. Nor was the Doctor happier in his selection, when he told the old, ever new and curious story of the waning of a woman's love, seeking strange, new channels, only to return to its legitimate source after days of fierce unrest. It was one of the many little human documents which had been unfolded to him during his long career as a physician. The story did not seem especially to impress Edna. She had one of her own to tell, of a woman who paddled away with her lover one night in a pirogue and never came back. They were lost amid the Baratarian Islands, and no one ever heard of them or found trace of them from that day to this. It was a pure invention. She said that Madame Antoine had related it to her. That, also, was an invention. Perhaps it was a dream she had had. But every glowing word seemed real to those who listened. They could feel the hot breath of the Southern night; they could hear the long sweep of the pirogue through the glistening moonlit water, the beating of bird's wings, rising startled from among the reeds in the salt-water pools; they could see the faces of the lovers, pale, close together, rapt in oblivious forgetfulness, drifting into the unknown.

The champagne was cold, and its subtle fumes played fantastic tricks with Edna's memory that night.

Outside, away from the glow of the fire and the soft lamplight, the night was chill and murky. The Doctor doubled his old-fashioned cloak across his breast as he strode home through the darkness. He knew his fellow creatures better than most men, knew that inner life which so seldom unfolds itself to unanointed eyes. He was sorry he had accepted Pontellier's invitation. He was growing old, and beginning to need rest and an unperturbed spirit. He did not want the secrets of other lives thrust upon him.

'I hope it isn't Arobin,' he muttered to himself as he walked. 'I hope to heaven it isn't Alcée Arobin.'

XXIV

Edna and her father had a warm, and almost violent dispute upon the subject of her refusal to attend her sister's wedding. Mr Pontellier declined to interfere, to interpose either his influence or his authority. He was following Doctor Mandelet's advice, and letting her do as she liked. The Colonel reproached his daughter for her lack of filial kindness and respect, her want of sisterly affection and womanly consideration. His arguments were labored and unconvincing. He doubted if Janet would accept any excuse – forgetting that Edna had offered none. He doubted if Janet would ever speak to her again, and he was sure Margaret would not.

Edna was glad to be rid of her father when he finally took himself off with his wedding garments and his bridal gifts, with his padded shoulders, his Bible reading, his 'toddies' and ponderous oaths.

Mr Pontellier followed him closely. He meant to stop at the wedding on his way to New York and endeavor by every means which money and love could devise to atone somewhat for Edna's incomprehensible action.

'You are too lenient, too lenient by far, Léonce,' asserted the Colonel. 'Authority, coercion are what is needed. Put your foot down good and hard; the only way to manage a wife. Take my word for it.'

The Colonel was perhaps unaware that he had coerced his own wife into her grave. Mr Pontellier had a vague suspicion of it which he thought it needless to mention at that late day.

Edna was not so consciously gratified at her husband's leaving home as she had been over the departure of her father. As the day approached when he was to leave her for a comparatively long stay, she grew melting and affectionate, remembering his many acts of consideration and his repeated expressions of an ardent attachment. She was solicitous about his health and his welfare. She bustled around, looking after his clothing, thinking about heavy underwear, quite as Madame Ratignolle would have done under similar circumstances. She cried when he went away, calling him her dear, good friend, and she was quite certain she would grow lonely before very long and go to join him in New York.

But after all, a radiant peace settled upon her when she at last found herself alone. Even the children were gone. Old Madame Pontellier had come herself and carried them off to Iberville with their quadroon. The old madame did not venture to say she was afraid they would be neglected during Léonce's absence; she hardly ventured to think so. She was hungry for them – even a little fierce in her attachment. She did not want them to be wholly 'children of the pavement,' she always said when begging to have them for a space. She wished them to know the country, with its streams, its fields, its woods, its freedom, so delicious to the young. She wished them to taste something of the life their father had lived and known and loved when he, too, was a little child.

When Edna was at last alone, she breathed a big, genuine sigh of relief. A feeling that was unfamiliar but very delicious came over her. She walked all through the house, from one room to another, as if inspecting it for the first time. She tried the various chairs and lounges, as if she had never sat and reclined upon them before. And she perambulated around the outside of the house, investigating, looking to see if windows and shutters were secure and in order. The flowers were like new acquaintances; she approached them in a familiar spirit, and made herself at home among them. The garden walks were damp, and Edna called to the maid to bring out her rubber sandals. And there she stayed, and stooped, digging around the plants, trimming, picking dead, dry leaves. The children's little dog came out, interfering, getting in her way. She scolded him, laughed at him, played with him. The garden smelled so good and looked so pretty in the afternoon sunlight. Edna plucked all the bright flowers she could find, and went into the house with them, she and the little dog.

Even the kitchen assumed a sudden interesting character which she had never before perceived. She went in to give directions to the cook, to say that the butcher would have to bring much less meat, that they would require only half their usual quantity of bread, of milk and groceries. She told the cook that she herself would be greatly occupied during Mr Pontellier's absence, and she begged her to take all thought and responsibility of the larder upon her own shoulders.

That night Edna dined alone. The candelabra, with a few candles in the center of the table, gave all the light she needed. Outside the circle of light in which she sat, the large dining room looked solemn and shadowy. The cook, placed upon her mettle, served a delicious repast – a luscious tender-loin broiled *à point*. The wine tasted good; the *marron glacé* seemed to be just what she wanted. It was so pleasant, too, to dine in a comfortable *peignoir*.

She thought a little sentimentally about Léonce and the children, and wondered what they were doing. As she gave a dainty scrap or two to the doggie, she talked intimately to him about Étienne and Raoul. He was beside himself with astonish-ment and delight over these companionable advances, and showed his appreciation by his little quick, snappy barks and a lively agitation.

Then Edna sat in the library after dinner and read Emerson until she grew sleepy. She realized that she had neglected her reading, and determined to start anew upon a course of improving studies, now that her time was completely her own to do with as she liked.

After a refreshing bath, Edna went to bed. And as she snuggled comfortably beneath the eiderdown a sense of restfulness invaded her, such as she had not known before.

XXV

When the weather was dark and cloudy Edna could not work. She needed the sun to mellow and temper her mood to the sticking point. She had reached a stage when she seemed to be no longer feeling her way, working, when in the humor, with sureness and ease. And being devoid of ambition, and striving not toward accomplishment, she drew satisfaction from the work in itself.

On rainy or melancholy days Edna went out and sought the society of the friends she had made at Grand Isle. Or else she stayed indoors and nursed a mood with which she was becoming too familiar for her own comfort and peace of mind. It was not despair, but it seemed to her as if life were passing by, leaving its promise broken and unfulfilled. Yet there were other days when she listened, was led on and deceived by fresh promises which her youth held out to her.

She went again to the races, and again. Alcée Arobin and Mrs Highcamp called for her one bright afternoon in Arobin's drag. Mrs Highcamp was a worldly but unaffected, intelligent, slim, tall blonde woman in the forties, with an indifferent manner and blue eyes that stared. She had a daughter who served her as a pretext for cultivating the society of young men of fashion. Alcée Arobin was one of them. He was a familiar figure at the race course, the opera, the fashionable clubs. There was a perpetual smile in his eyes, which seldom failed to awaken a corresponding cheerfulness in any one who looked into them and listened to his good-humored voice. His manner was quiet, and at times a little insolent. He possessed a good figure, a pleasing face, not overburdened with depth of thought or feeling; and his dress was that of the conventional man of fashion.

He admired Edna extravagantly, after meeting her at the races with her father. He had met her before on other occasions, but she had seemed to him unapproachable until that day. It was at his instigation that Mrs Highcamp called to ask her to go with them to the Jockey Club to witness the turf event of the season.

There were possibly a few track men out there who knew the race horse as well as Edna, but there was certainly none who knew it better. She sat between her two companions as one having author-ity to speak. She laughed at Arobin's pretensions, and deplored Mrs Highcamp's ignorance. The race horse was a friend and intimate associate of her childhood. The atmosphere of the stables and the breath of the bluegrass paddock revived in her memory and lingered in her nostrils. She did not perceive that she was talking like her father as the sleek geldings ambled in review before them. She played for very high stakes, and fortune favored her.

The fever of the game flamed in her cheeks and eyes, and it got into her blood and into her brain like an intoxicant. People turned their heads to look at her, and more than one lent an attentive ear to her utterances, hoping thereby to secure the elusive but ever-desired 'tip.' Arobin caught the contagion of excitement which drew him to Edna like a magnet. Mrs Highcamp remained, as usual, unmoved, with her indifferent stare and uplifted eyebrows.

Edna stayed and dined with Mrs Highcamp upon being urged to do so. Arobin also remained and sent away his drag.

The dinner was quiet and uninteresting, save for the cheerful efforts of Arobin to enliven things. Mrs Highcamp deplored the absence of her daughter from the races, and tried to convey to her what she had missed by going to the 'Dante reading' instead of joining them. The girl held a geranium leaf up to her nose and said nothing, but looked knowing and noncommittal. Mr Highcamp was a plain, bald-headed man, who only talked under compulsion. He was unresponsive. Mrs Highcamp was full of delicate courtesy and consideration toward her husband. She addressed most of her conversation to him at table. They sat in the library after dinner and read the evening papers together under the droplight, while the younger people went into the drawing room near by and talked. Miss Highcamp played some selections from Grieg upon the piano. She seemed to have apprehended all of the composer's coldness and none of his poetry. While Edna listened she could not help wondering if she had lost her taste for music.

When the time came for her to go home, Mr Highcamp grunted a lame offer to escort her, looking down at his slippered feet with tactless concern. It was Arobin who took her home. The car ride was long, and it was late when they reached Esplanade Street. Arobin asked permission to enter for a second to light his cigarette – his match safe was empty. He filled his match safe, but did not light his cigarette until he left her, after she had expressed her willingness to go to the races with him again.

Edna was neither tired nor sleepy. She was hungry again, for the Highcamp dinner, though of excellent quality, had lacked abundance. She rummaged in the larder and brought forth a slice of 'Gruyère' and some crackers. She opened a bottle of beer which she found in the icebox. Edna felt extremely restless and excited. She vacantly hummed a fantastic tune as she poked at the wood embers on the hearth and munched a cracker.

She wanted something to happen – something, anything; she did not know what. She regretted that she had not made Arobin stay a half hour to talk over the horses with her. She counted the money she had won. But there was nothing else to do, so she went to bed, and tossed there for hours in a sort of monotonous agitation.

In the middle of the night she remembered that

she had forgotten to write her regular letter to her husband; and she decided to do so next day and tell him about her afternoon at the Jockey Club. She lay wide awake composing a letter which was nothing like the one which she wrote next day. When the maid awoke her in the morning Edna was dreaming of Mr Highcamp playing the piano at the entrance of a music store on Canal Street, while his wife was saying to Alcée Arobin, as they boarded an Esplan-ade Street car:

'What a pity that so much talent has been neglected! but I must go.'

When, a few days later, Alcée Arobin again called for Edna in his drag, Mrs Highcamp was not with him. He said they would pick her up. But as that lady had not been apprised of his intention of picking her up, she was not at home. The daughter was just leaving the house to attend the meeting of a branch Folk Lore Society, and regretted that she could not accompany them. Arobin appeared non-plussed, and asked Edna if there were any one else she cared to ask.

She did not deem it worth while to go in search of any of the fashionable acquaintances from whom she had withdrawn herself. She thought of Madame Ratignolle, but knew that her fair friend did not leave the house, except to take a languid walk around the block with her husband after nightfall. Mademoiselle Reisz would have laughed at such a request from Edna. Madame Lebrun might have enjoyed the outing, but for some reason Edna did not want her. So they went alone, she and Arobin.

The afternoon was intensely interesting to her. The excitement came back upon her like a remittent fever. Her talk grew familiar and confidential. It was no labor to become intimate with Arobin. His manner invited easy confidence. The preliminary stage of becoming acquainted was one which he always endeavored to ignore when a pretty and engaging woman was concerned.

He stayed and dined with Edna. He stayed and sat beside the wood fire. They laughed and talked; and before it was time to go he was telling her how different life might have been if he had known her years before. With ingenuous frankness he spoke of what a wicked, ill-disciplined boy he had been, and impulsively drew up his cuff to exhibit upon his wrist the scar from a saber cut which he had received in a duel outside of Paris when he was nineteen. She touched his hand as she scanned the red cicatrice on the inside of his white wrist. A quick impulse that was somewhat spasmodic impelled her fingers to close in a sort of clutch upon his hand. He felt the pressure of her pointed nails in the flesh of his palm.

She arose hastily and walked toward the mantel.

'The sight of a wound or scar always agitates and sickens me,' she said. 'I shouldn't have looked at it.'

'I beg your pardon,' he entreated, following her; 'it never occurred to me that it might be repulsive.'

He stood close to her, and the effrontery in his

eyes repelled the old, vanishing self in her, yet drew all her awakening sensuousness. He saw enough in her face to impel him to take her hand and hold it while he said his lingering good night.

'Will you go to the races again?' he asked.

'No,' she said. 'I've had enough of the races. I don't want to lose all the money I've won, and I've got to work when the weather is bright, instead of – '

'Yes; work; to be sure. You promised to show me your work. What morning may I come up to your atelier? Tomorrow?'

'No!'

'Day after?'

'No, no.'

'Oh, please don't refuse me! I know something of such things. I might help you with a stray suggestion or two.'

'No. Good night. Why don't you go after you have said good night? I don't like you,' she went on in a high, excited pitch, attempting to draw away her hand. She felt that her words lacked dignity and sincerity, and she knew that he felt it.

'I'm sorry you don't like me. I'm sorry I offended you. How have I offended you? What have I done? Can't you forgive me?' And he bent and pressed his lips upon her hand as if he wished never more to withdraw them.

'Mr Arobin,' she complained, 'I'm greatly upset by the excitement of the afternoon; I'm not myself. My manner must have misled you in some way. I

146

wish you to go, please.' She spoke in a monotonous dull tone. He took his hat from the table, and stood with eyes turned from her, looking into the dying fire. For a moment or two he kept an impressive silence.

'Your manner has not misled me, Mrs Pontellier,' he said finally. 'My own emotions have done that. I couldn't help it. When I'm near you, how could I help it? Don't think anything of it, don't bother, please. You see, I go when you command me. If you wish me to stay away, I shall do so. If you let me come back, I – oh! you will let me come back?'

He cast one appealing glance at her, to which she made no response. Alcée Arobin's manner was so genuine that it often deceived even himself.

Edna did not care or think whether it were genuine or not. When she was alone she looked mechanically at the back of her hand which he had kissed so warmly. Then she leaned her head down on the mantelpiece. She felt somewhat like a woman who in a moment of passion is betrayed into an act of infidelity, and realizes the significance of the act without being wholly awakened from its glamour. The thought was passing vaguely through her mind, 'What would he think?'

She did not mean her husband; she was thinking of Robert Lebrun. Her husband seemed to her now like a person whom she had married without love as an excuse.

She lit a candle and went up to her room. Alcée Arobin was absolutely nothing to her. Yet his presence, his manners, the warmth of his glances, and above all the touch of his lips upon her hand had acted like a narcotic upon her.

She slept a languorous sleep, interwoven with vanishing dreams.

XXVI

Alcée Arobin wrote Edna an elaborate note of apology, palpitant with sincerity. It embarrassed her, for in a cooler, quieter moment it appeared to her absurd that she should have taken his action so seriously, so dramatically. She felt sure that the significance of the whole occurrence had lain in her own self-consciousness. If she ignored his note it would give undue importance to a trivial affair. If she replied to it in a serious spirit it would still leave in his mind the impression that she had in a susceptible moment yielded to his influence. After all, it was no great matter to have one's hand kissed. She was provoked at his having written the apology. She answered in as light and bantering a spirit as she fancied it deserved, and said she would be glad to have him look in upon her at work whenever he felt the inclination and his business gave him the opportunity.

He responded at once by presenting himself at her home with all his disarming naïveté. And then there was scarcely a day which followed that she did not see him or was not reminded of him. He was prolific in pretexts. His attitude became one of good-humored subservience and tacit adoration. He was ready at all times to submit to her moods, which were as often kind as they were cold. She grew accustomed to him. They became intimate and friendly by imperceptible degrees, and then by leaps. He sometimes talked in a way that astonished her at first and brought the crimson into her face; in a way that pleased her at last, appealing to the animalism that stirred impatiently within her.

There was nothing which so quieted the turmoil of Edna's senses as a visit to Mademoiselle Reisz. It was then, in the presence of that personality which was offensive to her, that the woman, by her divine art, seemed to reach Edna's spirit and set it free.

It was misty, with heavy, lowering atmosphere, one afternoon, when Edna climbed the stairs to the pianist's apartments under the roof. Her clothes were dripping with moisture. She felt chilled and pinched as she entered the room. Mademoiselle was poking at a rusty stove that smoked a little and warmed the room indifferently. She was endeavoring to heat a pot of chocolate on the stove. The room looked cheerless and dingy to Edna as she entered. A bust of Beethoven, covered with a hood of dust, scowled at her from the mantelpiece.

'Ah! here comes the sunlight!' exclaimed Mademoiselle, rising from her knees before the stove. 'Now it will be warm and bright enough; I can let the fire alone.'

She closed the stove door with a bang, and approaching, assisted in removing Edna's dripping mackintosh.

'You are cold; you look miserable. The chocolate

will soon be hot. But would you rather have a taste of brandy? I have scarcely touched the bottle which you brought me for my cold.' A piece of red flannel was wrapped around Mademoiselle's throat; a stiff neck compelled her to hold her head on one side.

'I will take some brandy,' said Edna, shivering as she removed her gloves and overshoes. She drank the liquor from the glass as a man would have done. Then flinging herself upon the uncomfortable sofa she said, 'Mademoiselle, I am going to move away from my house on Esplanade Street.'

'Ah!' ejaculated the musician, neither surprised nor especially interested. Nothing ever seemed to astonish her very much. She was endeavoring to adjust the bunch of violets which had become loose from its fastening in her hair. Edna drew her down upon the sofa, and taking a pin from her own hair, secured the shabby artificial flowers in their accustomed place.

'Aren't you astonished?'

'Passably. Where are you going? to New York? to Iberville? to your father in Mississippi? where?'

'Just two steps away,' laughed Edna, 'in a little four-room house around the corner. It looks so cozy, so inviting and restful, whenever I pass by; and it's for rent. I'm tired looking after that big house. It never seemed like mine, anyway – like home. It's too much trouble. I have to keep too many servants. I am tired bothering with them.'

'That is not your true reason, *ma belle*. There is no use in telling me lies. I don't know your reason, but you have not told me the truth.' Edna did not protest or endeavor to justify herself.

'The house, the money that provides for it, are not mine. Isn't that enough reason?'

'They are your husband's,' returned Mademoiselle, with a shrug and a malicious elevation of the eyebrows.

'Oh! I see there is no deceiving you. Then let me tell you: It is a caprice. I have a little money of my own from my mother's estate, which my father sends me by driblets. I won a large sum this winter on the races, and I am beginning to sell my sketches. Laidpore is more and more pleased with my work; he says it grows in force and individuality. I cannot judge of that myself, but I feel that I have gained in ease and confidence. However, as I said, I have sold a good many through Laidpore. I can live in the tiny house for little or nothing, with one servant. Old Celestine, who works occasionally for me, says she will come stay with me and do my work. I know I shall like it, like the feeling of freedom and independence.'

'What does your husband say?'

'I have not told him yet. I only thought of it this morning. He will think I am demented, no doubt. Perhaps you think so.'

Mademoiselle shook her head slowly. 'Your reason is not yet clear to me,' she said.

Neither was it quite clear to Edna herself; but it unfolded itself as she sat for a while in silence. Instinct had prompted her to put away her husband's bounty in casting off her allegiance. She did not know how it would be when he returned. There would have to be an understanding, an explanation. Conditions would some way adjust themselves, she felt; but whatever came, she had resolved never again to belong to another than herself.

'I shall give a grand dinner before I leave the old house!' Edna exclaimed. 'You will have to come to it, Mademoiselle. I will give you everything that you like to eat and drink. We shall sing and laugh and be merry for once.' And she uttered a sigh that came from the very depths of her being.

If Mademoiselle happened to have received a letter from Robert during the interval of Edna's visits, she would give her the letter unsolicited. And she would seat herself at the piano and play as her humor prompted her while the young woman read the letter.

The little stove was roaring; it was redhot, and the chocolate in the tin sizzled and sputtered. Edna went forward and opened the stove door, and Mademoiselle rising, took a letter from under the bust of Beethoven and handed it to Edna.

'Another! so soon!' she exclaimed, her eyes filled with delight. 'Tell me, Mademoiselle, does he know that I see his letters?'

'Never in the world! He would be angry and would never write to me again if he thought so. Does he write to you? Never a line. Does he send you a message? Never a word. It is because he loves you, poor fool, and is trying to forget you, since you are not free to listen to him or to belong to him.'

'Why do you show me his letters, then?'

'Haven't you begged for them? Can I refuse you anything? Oh! you cannot deceive me,' and Mademoiselle approached her beloved instrument and began to play. Edna did not at once read the letter. She sat holding it in her hand, while the music penetrated her whole being like an effulgence, warming and brightening the dark places of her soul. It prepared her for joy and exultation.

'Oh!' she exclaimed, letting the letter fall to the floor. 'Why did you not tell me?' She went and grasped Mademoiselle's hands up from the keys. 'Oh! unkind! malicious! Why did you not tell me?'

'That he was coming back? No great news, *ma foi*. I wonder he did not come long ago.'

'But when, when?' cried Edna, impatiently. 'He does not say when.'

'He says "very soon." You know as much about it as I do; it is all in the letter.'

'But why? Why is he coming? Oh, if I thought – ' and she snatched the letter from the floor and turned the pages this way and that way, looking for the reason, which was left untold.

'If I were young and in love with a man,' said Mademoiselle, turning on the stool and pressing her wiry hands between her knees as she looked down at Edna, who sat on the floor holding the letter, 'it seems to me he would have to be some *grand esprit*, a man with lofty aims and ability to reach them; one who stood high enough to attract the notice of his fellow-men. It seems to me if I were young and in love I should never deem a man of ordinary caliber worthy of my devotion.'

'Now it is you who are telling lies and seeking to deceive me, Mademoiselle; or else you have never been in love, and know nothing about it. Why,' went on Edna, clasping her knees and looking up into Mademoiselle's twisted face, 'do you suppose a woman knows why she loves? Does she select? Does she say to herself: "Go to! Here is a distinguished statesman with presidential possibilities; I shall proceed to fall in love with him." Or, "I shall set my heart upon this musician, whose fame is on every tongue?" Or, "This financier, who controls the world's money markets?"'

'You are purposely misunderstanding me, *ma reine*. Are you in love with Robert?'

'Yes,' said Edna. It was the first time she had admitted it, and a glow overspread her face, blotching it with red spots.

'Why?' asked her companion 'Why do you love him when you ought not to?'

Edna, with a motion or two, dragged herself on her knees before Mademoiselle Reisz, who took the glowing face between her two hands.

'Why? Because his hair is brown and grows away from his temples; because he opens and shuts his eyes, and his nose is a little out of drawing, because he has two lips and a square chin, and a little finger which he can't straighten from having played base-ball too energetically in his youth. Because – '

'Because you do, in short,' laughed Mademoiselle. 'What will you do when he comes back?' she asked.

'Do? Nothing, except feel glad and happy to be alive.'

She was already glad and happy to be alive at the mere thought of his return. The murky, lowering sky, which had depressed her a few hours before, seemed bracing and invigorating as she splashed through the streets on her way home.

She stopped at a confectioner's and ordered a huge box of bonbons for the children in Iberville. She slipped a card in the box, on which she scribbled a tender message and sent an abundance of kisses.

Before dinner in the evening Edna wrote a charming letter to her husband, telling him of her intention to move for a while into the little house around the block, and to give a farewell dinner before leaving, regretting that he was not there to share it, to help her out with the menu and assist her in entertaining the guests. Her letter was brilliant and brimming with cheerfulness.

XXVII

'What is the matter with you?' asked Arobin that evening. 'I never found you in such a happy mood.' Edna was tired by that time, and was reclining on the lounge before the fire.

'Don't you know the weather prophet has told us we shall see the sun pretty soon?'

'Well, that ought to be reason enough,' he acquiesced. 'You wouldn't give me another if I sat here all night imploring you.' He sat close to her on a low tabouret, and as he spoke his fingers lightly touched the hair that fell a little over her forehead. She liked the touch of his fingers through her hair, and closed her eyes sensitively.

'One of these days,' she said, 'I'm going to pull myself together for a while and think – try to determine what character of a woman I am, for, candidly, I don't know. By all the codes which I am acquainted with, I am a devilishly wicked specimen of the sex. But some way I can't convince myself that I am. I must think about it.'

'Don't. What's the use? Why should you bother thinking about it when I can tell you what manner of woman you are.' His fingers strayed occasionally down to her warm, smooth cheeks and firm chin, which was growing a little full and double.

'Oh, yes! You will tell me that I am adorable, everything that is captivating. Spare yourself the effort.'

'No, I shan't tell you anything of the sort, though I shouldn't be lying if I did.'

'Do you know Mademoiselle Reisz?' she asked irrelevantly.

'The pianist? I know her by sight. I've heard her play.'

'She says queer things sometimes in a bantering way that you don't notice at the time and you find yourself thinking about afterward.'

'For instance?'

'Well, for instance, when I left her today, she put her arms around me and felt my shoulder blades, to see if my wings were strong, she said. "The bird that would soar above the level plain of tradition and prejudice must have strong wings. It is a sad spectacle to see the weaklings bruised, exhausted, fluttering back to earth."'

'Whither would you soar?'

'I'm not thinking of any extraordinary flights. I only half comprehend her.'

'I've heard she's partially demented,' said Arobin.

'She seems to me wonderfully sane,' Edna replied.

'I'm told she's extremely disagreeable and unpleasant. Why have you introduced her at a moment when I desired to talk of you?'

'Oh! talk of me if you like,' cried Edna, clasping

her hands beneath her head; 'but let me think of something else while you do.'

'I'm jealous of your thoughts tonight. They're making you a little kinder than usual, but some way I feel as if they were wandering, as if they were not here with me.' She only looked at him and smiled. His eyes were very near. He leaned upon the lounge with an arm extended across her, while the other hand still rested upon her hair. They continued silently to look into each other's eyes. When he leaned forward and kissed her, she clasped his head, holding his lips to hers.

It was the first kiss of her life to which her nature had really responded. It was a flaming torch that kindled desire.

XXVIII

Edna cried a little that night after Arobin left her. It was only one phase of the multitudinous emotions which had assailed her. There was with her an overwhelming feeling of irresponsibility. There was the shock of the unexpected and the unaccustomed. There was her husband's reproach looking at her from the external things around her which he had provided for her external existence. There was Robert's reproach making itself felt by a quicker, fiercer, more overpowering love, which had awakened within her toward him. Above all, there was understanding. She felt as if a mist had been lifted from her eyes, enabling her to look upon and comprehend the significance of life, that monster made up of beauty and brutality. But among the conflicting sensations which assailed her, there was neither shame nor remorse. There was a dull pang of regret because it was not the kiss of love which had inflamed her, because it was not love which had held this cup of life to her lips.

XXIX

Without even waiting for an answer from her husband regarding his opinion or wishes in the matter, Edna hastened her preparations for quitting her home on Esplanade Street and moving into the little house around the block. A feverish anxiety attended her every action in that direction. There was no moment of deliberation, no interval of repose between the thought and its fulfillment. Early upon the morning following those hours passed in Arobin's society, Edna set about securing her new abode and hurrying her arrangements for occupying it. Within the precincts of her home she felt like one who has entered and lingered within the portals of some forbidden temple in which a thousand muffled voices bade her begone.

Whatever was her own in the house, everything which she had acquired aside from her husband's bounty, she caused to be transported to the other house, supplying simple and meager deficiencies from her own resources.

Arobin found her with rolled sleeves, working in company with the house maid when he looked in during the afternoon. She was splendid and robust, and had never appeared handsomer than in the old blue gown, with a red silk handkerchief knotted at random around her head to protect her hair from the dust. She was mounted upon a high stepladder, unhooking a picture from the wall when he entered. He had found the front door open, and had followed his ring by walking in unceremoniously.

'Come down!' he said. 'Do you want to kill yourself?' She greeted him with affected careless-ness, and appeared absorbed in her occupation.

If he had expected to find her languishing, reproachful, or indulging in sentimental tears, he must have been greatly surprised.

He was no doubt prepared for any emergency, ready for any one of the foregoing attitudes, just as he bent himself easily and naturally to the situation which confronted him.

'Please come down,' he insisted, holding the ladder and looking up at her.

'No,' she answered; 'Ellen is afraid to mount the ladder. Joe is working over at the "pigeon house" – that's the name Ellen gives it, because it's so small and looks like a pigeon house – and someone has to do this.'

Arobin pulled off his coat, and expressed himself ready and willing to tempt fate in her place. Ellen brought him one of her dust-caps, and went into contortions of mirth, which she found it impossible to control, when she saw him put it on before the mirror as grotesquely as he could. Edna herself could not refrain from smiling when she fastened it at his request. So it was he who in turn mounted the ladder, unhooking pictures and curtains, and dislodging ornaments as Edna directed. When he had finished he took off his dust-cap and went out to wash his hands.

Edna was sitting on the tabouret, idly brushing the tips of a feather duster along the carpet when he came in again.

'Is there anything more you will let me do?' he asked.

'That is all,' she answered. 'Ellen can manage the rest.' She kept the young woman occupied in the drawing-room, unwilling to be left alone with Arobin.

'What about the dinner?' he asked; 'the grand event, the *coup d'état?*'

'It will be a day after tomorrow. Why do you call it the "*coup d'état?*" Oh! it will be very fine; all my best of everything – crystal, silver and gold. Sèvres, flowers, music, and champagne to swim in. I'll let Léonce pay the bills. I wonder what he'll say when he sees the bills.'

'And you ask me why I call it a *coup d'état?*' Arobin had put on his coat, and he stood before her and asked if his cravat was plumb. She told him it was, looking no higher than the tip of his collar.

'When do you go to the "pigeon house?" – with all due acknowledgment to Ellen.'

'Day after tomorrow, after the dinner. I shall sleep there.'

'Ellen, will you very kindly get me a glass of water?' asked Arobin. 'The dust in the curtains, if you will pardon me for hinting such a thing, has parched my throat to a crisp.'

'While Ellen gets the water,' said Edna, rising, 'I will say good-by and let you go. I must get rid of this grime, and I have a million things to do and think of.'

'When shall I see you?' asked Arobin, seeking to detain her, the maid having left the room.'

'At the dinner, of course. You are invited.'

'Not before? – not tonight or tomorrow morning or tomorrow noon or night? or the day after morning or noon? Can't you see yourself, without my telling you, what an eternity it is?'

He had followed her into the hall and to the foot of the stairway, looking up at her as she mounted with her face half turned to him.

'Not an instant sooner,' she said. But she laughed and looked at him with eyes that at once gave him courage to wait and made it torture to wait.

XXX

Though Edna had spoken of the dinner as a very grand affair, it was in truth a very small affair and very select, in so much as the guests invited were few and were selected with discrimination. She had counted upon an even dozen seating themselves at her round mahogany board, forgetting for the moment that Madame Ratignolle was to the last degree *souffrante*[21] and unpresentable, and not foreseeing that Madame Lebrun would send a thousand regrets at the last moment. So there were only ten, after all, which made a cozy, comfortable number.

There were Mr and and Mrs Merriman, a pretty, vivacious little woman in the thirties; her husband, a jovial fellow, something of a shallow-pate, who laughed a good deal at other people's witticisms, and had thereby made himself extremely popular. Mrs Highcamp had accompanied them. Of course, there was Alcée Arobin, and Mademoiselle Reisz had consented to come. Edna had sent her a fresh bunch of violets with black lace trimmings for her hair. Monsieur Ratignolle brought himself and his wife's excuses. Victor Lebrun, who happened to be in the city, bent upon relaxation, had accepted with

21 In pain; in labor.

165

alacrity. There was a Miss Mayblunt, no longer in her teens, who looked at the world through lorgnettes and with the keenest interest. It was thought and said that she was intellectual; it was suspected of her that she wrote under a *nom de guerre*. She had come with a gentleman by the name of Gouvernail, connected with one of the daily papers, of whom nothing special could be said, except that he was observant and seemed quiet and inoffensive. Edna herself made the tenth, and at half-past eight they seated themselves at table, Arobin and Monsieur Ratignolle on either side of their hostess.

Mrs Highcamp sat between Arobin and Victor Lebrun. Then came Mrs Merriman, Mr Gouvernail, Miss Mayblunt, Mr Merriman, and Mademoiselle Reisz next to Monsieur Ratignolle.

There was something extremely gorgeous about the appearance of the table, an effect of splendor conveyed by a cover of pale yellow satin under strips of lace-work. There were wax candles in massive brass candelabra, burning softly under yellow silk shades; full, fragrant roses, yellow and red, abounded. There were silver and gold, as she had said there would be, and crystal which glittered like the gems which the women wore.

The ordinary stiff dining chairs had been discarded for the occasion and replaced by the most commodious and luxurious which could be collected throughout the house. Mademoiselle Reisz, being exceedingly diminutive, was elevated upon cushions, as small children are sometimes hoisted at table upon bulky volumes.

'Something new, Edna?' exclaimed Miss Mayblunt, with lorgnette directed toward a magnificent cluster of diamonds that sparkled, that almost sputtered, in Edna's hair, just over the center of her forehead.

'Quite new, "brand" new, in fact, a present from my husband. It arrived this morning from New York. I may as well admit that this is my birthday, and that I am twenty-nine. In good time I expect you to drink my health. Meanwhile, I shall ask you to begin with this cocktail, composed – would you say "composed?"' with an appeal to Miss Mayblunt – 'composed by my father in honor of Sister Janet's wedding.'

Before each guest stood a tiny glass that looked and sparkled like a garnet gem.

'Then, all things considered,' spoke Arobin, 'it might not be amiss to start out by drinking the Colonel's health in the cocktail which he composed, on the birthday of the most charming of women – the daughter whom he invented.'

Mr Merriman's laugh at this sally was such a genuine outburst and so contagious that it started the dinner with an agreeable swing that never slackened.

Miss Mayblunt begged to be allowed to keep her cocktail untouched before her, just to look at. The color was marvelous! She could compare it to nothing she had ever seen, and the garnet lights which it emitted were unspeakably rare. She pronounced the Colonel an artist, and stuck to it.

Monsieur Ratignolle was prepared to take things seriously; the *mets*, the *entre-mets*,[22] the service, the decorations, even the people. He looked up from his pompano and inquired of Arobin if he were related to the gentleman of that name who formed one of the firm of Laitner and Arobin, lawyers. The young man admitted that Laitner was a warm personal friend, who permitted Arobin's name to decorate the firm's letterheads and to appear upon a shingle that graced Perdido Street.

'There are so many inquisitive people and institutions abounding,' said Arobin, 'that one is really forced as a matter of convenience these days to assume the virtue of an occupation if he has it not.'

Monsieur Ratignolle stared a little, and turned to ask Mademoiselle Reisz if she considered the symphony concerts up to the standard which had been set the previous winter. Mademoiselle Reisz answered Monsieur Ratignolle in French, which Edna thought a little rude, under the circumstances, but characteristic. Mademoiselle had only disagreeable things to say of the symphony concerts, and insulting remarks to make of all the musicians of New Orleans, singly and collectively. All her interest seemed to be centered upon the delicacies placed before her.

Mr Merriman said that Mr Arobin's remark

22 The food, the side dishes.

about inquisitive people reminded him of a man from Waco the other day at the St Charles Hotel – but as Mr Merriman's stories were always lame and lacking point, his wife seldom permitted him to complete them. She interrupted him to ask if he remembered the name of the author whose book she had bought the week before to send to a friend in Geneva. She was talking 'books' with Mr Gouvernail and trying to draw from him his opinion upon current literary topics. Her husband told the story of the Waco man privately to Miss Mayblunt, who pretended to be greatly amused and to think it extremely clever.

Mrs Highcamp hung with languid but unaffected interest upon the warm and impetuous volubility of her left-hand neighbor, Victor Lebrun. Her attention was never for a moment withdrawn from him after seating herself at table; and when he turned to Mrs Merriman, who was prettier and more vivacious than Mrs Highcamp, she waited with easy indifference for an opportunity to reclaim his attention. There was the occasional sound of music, of mandolins, sufficiently removed to be an agreeable accompaniment rather than an interruption to the conversation. Outside the soft, monotonous splash of a fountain could be heard; the sound penetrated into the room with the heavy odor of jessamine that came through the open windows.

The golden shimmer of Edna's satin gown spread in rich folds on either side of her. There was a soft fall of lace encircling her shoulders. It was the color of her skin, without the glow, the myriad living tints that one may sometimes discover in vibrant flesh. There was something in her attitude, in her whole appearance when she leaned her head against the high-backed chair and spread her arms, which suggested the regal woman, the one who rules, who looks on, who stands alone.

But as she sat there amid her guests, she felt the old ennui overtaking her, the hopelessness which so often assailed her, which came upon her like an obsession, like something extraneous, independent of volition. It was something which announced itself; a chill breath that seemed to issue from some vast cavern wherein discords wailed. There came over her the acute longing which always summoned into her spiritual vision the presence of the beloved one, overpowering her at once with a sense of the unattainable.

The moments glided on, while a feeling of good fellowship passed around the circle like a mystic cord, holding and binding these people together with jest and laughter. Monsieur Ratignolle was the first to break the pleasant charm. At ten o'clock he excused himself. Madame Ratignolle was waiting for him at home. She was *bien souffrante,* and she was filled with vague dread, which only her husband's presence could allay.

Mademoiselle Reisz arose with Monsieur Ratignolle, who offered to escort her to the car. She had eaten well; she had tasted the good, rich wines, and they must have turned her head, for she bowed pleasantly to all as she withdrew from table. She kissed Edna upon the shoulder, and whispered: *'Bonne nuit, ma reine; soyez sage.'*[23] She had been a little bewildered upon rising, or rather, descending from her cushions, and Monsieur Ratignolle gallantly took her arm and led her away.

Mrs Highcamp was weaving a garland of roses, yellow and red. When she had finished the garland, she laid it lightly upon Victor's black curls. He was reclining far back in the luxurious chair, holding a glass of champagne to the light.

As if a magician's wand had touched him, the garland of roses transformed him into a vision of Oriental beauty. His cheeks were the color of crushed grapes, and his dusky eyes glowed with a languishing fire.

'*Sapristi!*' exclaimed Arobin.

But Mrs Highcamp had one more touch to add to the picture. She took from the back of her chair a white silken scarf, with which she had covered her shoulders in the early part of the evening. She draped it across the boy in graceful folds, and in a way to conceal his black, conventional evening dress. He did not seem to mind what she did to him, only smiled, showing a faint gleam of white teeth, while he continued to gaze with narrowing eyes at the light through his glass of champagne.

'Oh! to be able to paint in color rather than in

23 Goodnight, my queen; be good.

words!' exclaimed Miss Mayblunt, losing herself in a rhapsodic dream as she looked at him.

'"There was a graven image of Desire
Painted with red blood on a ground of gold."'

murmured Gouvernail, under his breath.

The effect of the wine upon Victor was to change his accustomed volubility into silence. He seemed to have abandoned himself to a reverie, and to be seeing pleasing visions in the amber bead.

'Sing,' entreated Mrs Highcamp. 'Won't you sing to us?'

'Let him alone,' said Arobin.

'He's posing,' offered Mr Merriman; 'let him have it out.'

'I believe he's paralyzed,' laughed Mrs Merriman. And leaning over the youth's chair, she took the glass from his hand and held it to his lips. He sipped the wine slowly, and when he had drained the glass she laid it upon the table and wiped his lips with her little filmy handkerchief.

'Yes, I'll sing for you,' he said, turning in his chair toward Mrs Highcamp. He clasped his hands behind his head, and looking up at the ceiling began to hum a little, trying his voice like a musician tuning an instrument. Then, looking at Edna, he began to sing:

'Ah! si tu savais!'

'Stop!' she cried, 'don't sing that. I don't want you to sing it,' and she laid her glass so impetuously and blindly upon the table as to shatter it against a carafe. The wine spilled over Arobin's legs and some of it trickled down upon Mrs Highcamp's black gauze gown. Victor had lost all idea of courtesy, or else he thought his hostess was not in earnest, for he laughed and went on:

> 'Ah! si tu savais
> Ce que tes yeux me disent' – [24]

'Oh! you mustn't! you mustn't,' exclaimed Edna, and pushing back her chair she got up, and going behind him placed her hand over his mouth. He kissed the soft palm that pressed upon his lips.

'No, no, I won't, Mrs Pontellier. I didn't know you meant it,' looking up at her with caressing eyes. The touch of his lips was like a pleasing sting to her hand. She lifted the garland of roses from his head and flung it across the room.

'Come, Victor; you've posed long enough. Give Mrs Highcamp her scarf.'

Mrs Highcamp undraped the scarf from about him with her own hands. Miss Mayblunt and Mr Gouvernail suddenly conceived the notion that it was time to say good night. And Mr and Mrs Merriman wondered how it could be so late.

Before parting from Victor, Mrs Highcamp

24 Ah! if you knew what your eyes say to me.

invited him to call upon her daughter, who she knew would be charmed to meet him and talk French and sing French songs with him. Victor expressed his desire and intention to call upon Miss Highcamp at the first opportunity which presented itself. He asked if Arobin were going his way. Arobin was not.

The mandolin players had long since stolen away. A profound stillness had fallen upon the broad, beautiful street. The voices of Edna's disbanding guests jarred like a discordant note upon the quiet harmony of the night.

XXXI

'Well?' questioned Arobin, who had remained with Edna after the others had departed.

'Well,' she reiterated, and stood up, stretching her arms, and feeling the need to relax her muscles after having been so long seated.

'What next?' he asked.

'The servants are all gone. They left when the musicians did. I have dismissed them. The house has to be closed and locked, and I shall trot around to the pigeon house, and shall send Celestine over in the morning to straighten things up.'

He looked around, and began to turn out some of the lights.

'What about upstairs?' he inquired.

'I think it is all right; but there may be a window or two unlatched. We had better look; you might take a candle and see. And bring me my wrap and hat on the foot of the bed in the middle room.'

He went up with the light, and Edna began closing doors and windows. She hated to shut in the smoke and the fumes of the wine. Arobin found her cape and hat, which he brought down and helped her to put on.

When everything was secured and the lights put out, they left through the front door, Arobin locking it and taking the key, which he carried for Edna. He helped her down the steps.

'Will you have a spray of jessamine?' he asked, breaking off a few blossoms as he passed.

'No; I don't want anything.'

She seemed disheartened, and had nothing to say. She took his arm, which he offered her, holding up the weight of her satin train with the other hand. She looked down, noticing the black line of his leg moving in and out so close to her against the yellow shimmer of her gown. There was the whistle of a railway train somewhere in the distance, and the midnight bells were ringing. They met no one in their short walk.

The 'pigeon-house' stood behind a locked gate, and a shallow *parterre* that had been somewhat neglected. There was a small front porch, upon which a long window and the front door opened. The door opened directly into the parlour; there was no side entry. Back in the yard was a room for servants, in which old Celestine had been ensconced.

Edna had left a lamp burning low upon the table. She had succeeded in making the room look habitable and homelike. There were some books on the table and a lounge near at hand. On the floor was a fresh matting, covered with a rug or two; and on the walls hung a few tasteful pictures. But the room was filled with flowers. These were a surprise to her. Arobin had sent them, and had had Celestine distribute them during Edna's absence. Her bedroom was adjoining, and across a small passage were the dining room and kitchen.

Edna seated herself with every appearance of discomfort.

'Are you tired?' he asked.

'Yes, and chilled, and miserable. I feel as if I had been wound up to a certain pitch – too tight – and something inside of me had snapped.' She rested her head against the table upon her bare arm.

'You want to rest,' he said, 'and to be quiet. I'll go; I'll leave you and let you rest.'

'Yes,' she replied.

He stood up beside her and smoothed her hair with his soft, magnetic hand. His touch conveyed to her a certain physical comfort. She could have fallen quietly asleep there if he had continued to pass his hand over her hair. He brushed the hair upward from the nape of her neck.

'I hope you will feel better and happier in the morning,' he said. 'You have tried to do too much in the past few days. The dinner was the last straw; you might have dispensed with it.'

'Yes,' she admitted, 'it was stupid.'

'No, it was delightful; but it has worn you out.'

His hand had strayed to her beautiful shoulders, and he could feel the response of her flesh to his touch. He seated himself beside her and kissed her lightly upon the shoulder.

'I thought you were going away,' she said, in an uneven voice.

'I am, after I have said good night.'

'Good night,' she murmured.

He did not answer, except to continue to caress her. He did not say good night until she had become supple to his gentle, seductive entreaties.

XXXII

When Mr Pontellier learned of his wife's intention to abandon her home and take up her residence elsewhere, he immediately wrote her a letter of unqualified disapproval and remonstrance. She had given reasons which he was unwilling to acknowledge as adequate. He hoped she had not acted upon her rash impulse; and he begged her to consider first, foremost, and above all else, what people would say. He was not dreaming of scandal when he uttered this warning; that was a thing which would never have entered into his mind to consider in connection with his wife's name or his own. He was simply thinking of his financial integrity. It might get noised about that the Pontelliers had met with reverses, and were forced to conduct their *ménage* on a humbler scale than heretofore. It might do incalculable mischief to his business prospects.

But remembering Edna's whimsical turn of mind of late, and foreseeing that she had immediately acted upon her impetuous determination, he grasped the situation with his usual promptness and handled it with his well-known business tact and cleverness.

The same mail which brought to Edna his letter of disapproval carried instructions – the most minute instructions – to a well-known architect concerning the remodeling of his home, changes which he had long contemplated, and which he desired carried forward during his temporary absence.

Expert and reliable packers and movers were engaged to convey the furniture, carpets, pictures – everything movable, in short – to places of security. And in an incredibly short time the Pontellier house was turned over to the artisans. There was to be an addition – a small snuggery; there was to be frescoing, and hardwood flooring was to be put into such rooms as had not yet been subjected to this improvement.

Furthermore, in one of the daily papers appeared a brief notice to the effect that Mr and Mrs Pontellier were contemplating a summer sojourn abroad, and that their handsome residence on Esplanade Street was undergoing sumptuous alterations, and would not be ready for occupancy until their return. Mr Pontellier had saved appearances!

Edna admired the skill of his maneuver, and avoided any occasion to balk his intentions. When the situation as set forth by Mr Pontellier was accepted and taken for granted, she was apparently satisfied that it should be so.

The pigeon-house pleased her. It at once assumed the intimate character of a home, while she herself invested it with a charm which it reflected like a warm glow. There was with her a feeling of having descended in the social scale, with a corresponding sense of having risen in the spiritual. Every step which she took toward relieving herself from obligations added to her strength and expansion as an individual. She began to look with her own eyes; to see and to apprehend the deeper undercurrent of life. No longer was she content to 'feed upon opinion' when her own soul had invited her.

After a little while, a few days, in fact, Edna went up and spent a week with her children in Iberville. They were delicious February days, with all the summer's promise hovering in the air.

How glad she was to see the children! She wept for very pleasure when she felt their little arms clasping her; their hard, ruddy cheeks pressed against her own glowing cheeks. She looked into their faces with hungry eyes that could not be satisfied with looking. And what stories they had to tell their mother! About the pigs, the cows, the mules! About riding to the mill behind Gluglu, fishing back in the lake with their Uncle Jasper, picking pecans with Lidie's little black brood, and hauling chips in their express wagon. It was a thousand times more fun to haul real chips for old lame Susie's real fire than to drag painted blocks along the banquette on Esplanade Street!

She went with them herself to see the pigs and the cows, to look at the darkies laying the cane, to thrash the pecan trees, and catch fish in the back lake. She lived with them a whole week long, giving them all of herself, and gathering and filling herself with their young existence. They listened, breathless, when she told them the house in Esplanade Street was crowded with workmen, hammering, nailing, sawing, and filling the place with clatter. They wanted to know where their bed was, what had been done with their rocking horse; and where did Joe sleep, and where had Ellen gone, and the cook? But, above all, they were fired with a desire to see the little house around the block. Was there any place to play? Were there any boys next door? Raoul, with pessimistic foreboding, was convinced that there were only girls next door. Where would they sleep, and where would papa sleep? She told them the fairies would fix it all right.

The old Madame was charmed with Edna's visit, and showered all manner of delicate attentions upon her. She was delighted to know that the Esplanade Street house was in a dismantled condition. It gave her the promise and pretext to keep the children indefinitely.

It was with a wrench and a pang that Edna left her children. She carried away with her the sound of their voices and the touch of their cheeks. All along the journey homeward their presence lingered with her like the memory of a delicious song. But by the time she had regained the city the song no longer echoed in her soul. She was again alone.

XXIII

It happened sometimes when Edna went to see Mademoiselle Reisz that the little musician was absent, giving a lesson or making some small necessary household purchase. The key was always left in a secret hiding place in the entry, which Edna knew. If Mademoiselle happened to be away, Edna would usually enter and wait for her return.

When she knocked at Mademoiselle Reisz's door one afternoon there was no response; so unlocking the door, as usual, she entered and found the apartment deserted, as she had expected. Her day had been quite filled up, and it was for a rest, for a refuge, and to talk about Robert, that she sought out her friend.

She had worked at her canvas – a young Italian character study – all the morning, completing the work without the model, but there had been many interruptions, some incident to her modest house-keeping, and others of a social nature.

Madame Ratignolle had dragged herself over, avoiding the too public thoroughfares, she said. She complained that Edna had neglected her much of late. Besides, she was consumed with curiosity to see the little house and the manner in which it was conducted. She wanted to hear all about the dinner party; Monsieur Ratignolle had left *so* early. What had happened after he left? The champagne and grapes which Edna sent over were *too* delicious. She had so little appetite; they had refreshed and toned her stomach. Where on earth was she going to put Mr Pontellier in that little house, and the boys? And then she made Edna promise to go to her when her hour of trial overtook her.

'At any time – any time of the day or night, dear,' Edna assured her.

Before leaving Madame Ratignolle said:

'In some way you seem to me like a child, Edna. You seem to act without a certain amount of reflection which is necessary in this life. That is the reason I want to say you mustn't mind if I advise you to be a little careful while you are living here alone. Why don't you have someone come and stay with you? Wouldn't Mademoiselle Reisz come?'

'No; she wouldn't wish to come, and I shouldn't want her always with me.'

'Well, the reason – you know how evil-minded the world is – someone was talking of Alcée Arobin visiting you. Of course, it wouldn't matter if Mr Arobin had not such a dreadful reputation. Monsieur Ratignolle was telling me that his attentions alone are considered enough to ruin a woman's name.'

'Does he boast of his successes?' asked Edna, indifferently, squinting at her picture.

'No, I think not. I believe he is a decent fellow as far as that goes. But his character is so well known among the men. I shan't be able to come back and see you; it was very, very imprudent today.'

'Mind the step!' cried Edna.

'Don't neglect me,' entreated Madame Ratignolle; 'and don't mind what I said about Arobin, or having someone to stay with you.'

'Of course not,' Edna laughed. 'You may say anything you like to me.' They kissed each other good-by. Madame Ratignolle had not far to go, and Edna stood on the porch a while watching her walk down the street.

Then in the afternoon Mrs Merriman and Mrs Highcamp had made their 'party call.' Edna felt that they might have dispensed with the formality. They had also come to invite her to play *vingt-et-un* one evening at Mrs Merriman's. She was asked to go early, to dinner, and Mr Merriman or Mr Arobin would take her home. Edna accepted in a half-hearted way. She sometimes felt very tired of Mrs Highcamp and Mrs Merriman.

Late in the afternoon she sought refuge with Mademoiselle Rcisz, and stayed there alone, waiting for her, feeling a kind of repose invade her with the very atmosphere of the shabby, unpretentious little room.

Edna sat at the window, which looked out over the housetops and across the river. The window frame was filled with pots of flowers, and she sat and picked the dry leaves from a rose geranium. The day was warm, and the breeze which blew from the river was very pleasant. She removed her hat and laid it on the piano. She went on picking the leaves and digging around the plants with her hat pin. Once she thought she heard Mademoiselle Reisz approaching. But it was a young black girl, who came in, bringing a small bundle of laundry, which she deposited in the adjoining room, and went away.

Edna seated herself at the piano, and softly picked out with one hand the bars of a piece of music which lay open before her. A half hour went by. There was the occasional sound of people going and coming in the lower hall. She was growing interested in her occupation of picking out the aria, when there was a second rap at the door. She vaguely wondered what these people did when they found Mademoiselle's door locked.

'Come in,' she called, turning her face toward the door. And this time it was Robert Lebrun who presented himself. She attempted to rise; she could not have done so without betraying the agitation which mastered her at sight of him, so she fell back upon the stool, only exclaiming, 'Why, Robert!'

He came and clasped her hand, seemingly without knowing what he was saying or doing.

'Mrs Pontellier! How do you happen – oh! how well you look! Is Mademoiselle Reisz not here? I never expected to see you.'

'When did you come back?' asked Edna in an unsteady voice, wiping her face with her handkerchief. She seemed ill at ease on the piano stool, and he begged her to take the chair by the window. She did so, mechanically, while he seated himself on the stool.

'I returned day before yesterday,' he answered, while he leaned his arm on the keys, bringing forth a crash of discordant sound.

'Day before yesterday!' she repeated, aloud; and went on thinking to herself, 'day before yesterday,' in a sort of an uncomprehending way. She had pictured him seeking her at the very first hour, and he had lived under the same sky since day before yesterday, while only by accident had he stumbled upon her. Mademoiselle must have lied when she said, 'Poor fool, he loves you.'

'Day before yesterday,' she repeated, breaking off a spray of Mademoiselle's geranium; 'then if you had not met me here today you wouldn't – when – that is, didn't you mean to come and see me?'

'Of course, I should have gone to see you. There have been so many things – ' he turned the leaves of Mademoiselle's music nervously. 'I started in at once yesterday with the old firm. After all there is as much chance for me here as there was there – that is, I might find it profitable some day. The Mexicans were not very congenial.'

So he had come back because the Mexicans were not congenial; because business was as profitable here as there; because of any reason, and not because he cared to be near her. She remembered the day she sat on the floor, turning the pages of his letter, seeking the reason which was left untold.

She had not noticed how he looked – only feeling

his presence; but she turned deliberately and observed him. After all, he had been absent but a few months, and was not changed. His hair – the color of hers – waved back from his temples in the same way as before. His skin was not more burned than it had been at Grand Isle. She found in his eyes, when he looked at her for one silent moment, the same tender caress, with an added warmth and entreaty which had not been there before – the same glance which had penetrated to the sleeping places of her soul and awakened them.

A hundred times Edna had pictured Robert's return, and imagined their first meeting. It was usually at her home, whither he had sought her out at once. She always fancied him expressing or betraying in some way his love for her. And here, the reality was that they sat ten feet apart, she at the window, crushing geranium leaves in her hand and smelling them, he twirling around on the piano stool, saying:

'I was very much surprised to hear of Mr Pontellier's absence; it's a wonder Mademoiselle Reisz did not tell me; and your moving – mother told me yesterday. I should think you would have gone to New York with him, or to Iberville with the children, rather than be bothered here with housekeeping. And you are going abroad, too, I hear. We shan't have you at Grand Isle next summer; it won't seem – do you see much of Mademoiselle Reisz? She often spoke of you in the few letters she wrote.'

'Do you remember that you promised to write to

me when you went away?' A flush overspread his whole face.

'I couldn't believe that my letters would be of any interest to you.'

'That is an excuse; it isn't the truth.' Edna reached for her hat on the piano. She adjusted it, sticking the hat pin through the heavy coil of hair with some deliberation.

'Are you not going to wait for Mademoiselle Reisz?' asked Robert.

'No; I have found when she is absent this long, she is liable not to come back till late.' She drew on her gloves, and Robert picked up his hat.

'Won't you wait for her?' asked Edna.

'Not if you think she will not be back till late,' adding, as if suddenly aware of some discourtesy in his speech, 'and I should miss the pleasure of walking home with you.' Edna locked the door and put the key back in its hiding place.

They went together, picking their way across muddy streets and sidewalks encumbered with the cheap display of small tradesmen. Part of the distance they rode in the car, and after disembarking, passed the Pontellier mansion, which looked broken and half torn asunder. Robert had never known the house, and looked at it with interest.

'I never knew you in your former home,' he remarked.

'I am glad you did not.'

'Why?' She did not answer. They went on around the corner, and it seemed as if her dreams were coming true after all, when he followed her into the little house.

'You must stay and dine with me, Robert. You see I am all alone, and it is so long since I have seen you. There is so much I want to ask you.'

She took off her hat and gloves. He stood irresolute, making some excuse about his mother who expected him; he even muttered something about an engagement. She struck a match and lit the lamp on the table; it was growing dusk. When he saw her face in the lamp-light, looking pained, with all the soft lines gone out of it, he threw his hat aside and seated himself.

'Oh! you know I want to stay if you will let me!' he exclaimed. All the softness came back. She laughed, and went and put her hand on his shoulder.

'This is the first moment you have seemed like the old Robert. I'll go tell Celestine.' She hurried away to tell Celestine to set an extra place. She even sent her off in search of some added delicacy which she had not thought of for herself. And she recommended great care in dripping the coffee and having the omelet done to a proper turn.

When she reëntered, Robert was turning over magazines, sketches, and things that lay upon the table in great disorder. He picked up a photograph, and exclaimed:

'Alcée Arobin! What on earth is his picture doing here?'

'I tried to make a sketch of his head one day,'

answered Edna, 'and he thought the photograph might help me. It was at the other house. I thought it had been left there. I must have packed it up with my drawing materials.'

'I should think you would give it back to him if you have finished with it.'

'Oh! I have a great many such photographs. I never think of returning them. They don't amount to anything.' Robert kept on looking at the picture.

'It seems to me – do you think his head worth drawing? Is he a friend of Mr Pontellier's? You never said you knew him.'

'He isn't a friend of Mr Pontellier's; he's a friend of mine. I always knew him – that is, it is only of late that I know him pretty well. But I'd rather talk about you, and know what you have been seeing and doing and feeling out there in Mexico.' Robert threw aside the picture.

'I've been seeing the waves and the white beach of Grand Isle, the quiet, grassy street of the *Chênière*, the old fort at Grande Terre. I've been working like a machine, and feeling like a lost soul. There was nothing interesting.'

She leaned her head upon her hand to shade her eyes from the light.

'And what have you been seeing and doing and feeling all these days?' he asked.

'I've been seeing the waves and the white beach of Grand Isle, the quiet, grassy street of the *Chênière Caminada*, the old sunny fort at Grande Terre. I've been working with a little more comprehension than a machine, and still feeling like a lost soul. There was nothing interesting.'

'Mrs Pontellier, you are cruel,' he said, with feeling, closing his eyes and resting his head back in his chair. They remained in silence till old Celestine announced dinner.

XXXIV

The dining room was very small. Edna's round mahogany would have almost filled it. As it was there was but a step or two from the little table to the kitchen, to the mantel, the small buffet, and the side door that opened out on the narrow brick-paved yard.

A certain degree of ceremony settled upon them with the announcement of dinner. There was no return to personalities. Robert related incidents of his sojourn in Mexico, and Edna talked of events likely to interest him, which had occurred during his absence. The dinner was of ordinary quality, except for the few delicacies which she had sent out to purchase. Old Celestine, with a bandana *tignon* twisted about her head, hobbled in and out, taking a personal interest in everything; and she lingered occasionally to talk patois with Robert, whom she had known as a boy.

He went out to a neighboring cigar stand to purchase cigarette papers, and when he came back he found that Celestine had served the black coffee in the parlor.

'Perhaps I shouldn't have come back,' he said. 'When you are tired of me, tell me to go.'

'You never tire me. You must have forgotten the

hours and hours at Grand Isle in which we grew accustomed to each other and used to being together.'

'I have forgotten nothing at Grand Isle,' he said, not looking at her, but rolling a cigarette. His tobacco pouch, which he laid upon the table, was a fantastic embroidered silk affair, evidently the handiwork of a woman.

'You used to carry your tobacco in a rubber pouch,' said Edna, picking up the pouch and examining the needlework.

'Yes; it was lost.'

'Where did you buy this one? In Mexico?'

'It was given to me by a Vera Cruz girl; they are very generous,' he replied, striking a match and lighting his cigarette.

'They are very handsome, I suppose, those Mexican women; very picturesque, with their black eyes and their lace scarfs.'

'Some are; others are hideous. Just as you find women everywhere.'

'What was she like – the one who gave you the pouch? You must have known her very well.'

'She was very ordinary. She wasn't of the slightest importance. I knew her well enough.'

'Did you visit at her house? Was it interesting? I should like to know and hear about the people you met, and the impressions they made on you.'

'There are some people who leave impressions not so lasting as the imprint of an oar upon the water.'

'Was she such a one?'

'It would be ungenerous for me to admit that she was of that order and kind.' He thrust the pouch back in his pocket, as if to put away the subject with the trifle which had brought it up.

Arobin dropped in with a message from Mrs Merriman, to say that the card party was postponed on account of the illness of one of her children.

'How do you do, Arobin?' said Robert, rising from the obscurity.

'Oh! Lebrun. To be sure! I heard yesterday you were back. How did they treat you down in Mexique?'

'Fairly well.'

'But not well enough to keep you there. Stunning girls, though, in Mexico. I thought I should never get away from Vera Cruz when I was down there a couple of years ago.'

'Did they embroider slippers and tobacco pouches and hatbands and things for you?' asked Edna.

'Oh! my! no! I didn't get so deep in their regard. I fear they made more impression on me than I made on them.'

'You were less fortunate than Robert, then.'

'I am always less fortunate than Robert. Has he been imparting tender confidences?'

'I've been imposing myself long enough,' said Robert, rising, and shaking hands with Edna. 'Please convey my regards to Mr Pontellier when you write.'

He shook hands with Arobin and went away.

'Fine fellow, that Lebrun,' said Arobin when Robert had gone. 'I never heard you speak of him.'

'I knew him last summer at Grand Isle,' she replied. 'Here is that photograph of yours. Don't you want it?'

'What do I want with it? Throw it away.' She threw it back on the table.

'I'm not going to Mrs Merriman's,' she said. 'If you see her, tell her so. But perhaps I had better write. I think I shall write now, and say that I am sorry her child is sick, and tell her not to count on me.'

'It would be a good scheme,' acquiesced Arobin. 'I don't blame you; stupid lot!'

Edna opened the blotter, and having procured paper and pen, began to write the note. Arobin lit a cigar and read the evening paper, which he had in his pocket.

'What is the date?' she asked. He told her.

'Will you mail this for me when you go out?'

'Certainly.' He read to her little bits out of the newspaper, while she straightened things on the table.

'What do you want to do?' he asked, throwing aside the paper. 'Do you want to go out for a walk or a drive or anything? It would be a fine night to drive.'

'No; I don't want to do anything but just be quiet. You go away and amuse yourself. Don't stay.'

'I'll go away if I must; but I shan't amuse myself. You know that I only live when I am near you.'

He stood up to bid her good night.

'Is that one of the things you always say to women?'

'I have said it before, but I don't think I ever came so near meaning it,' he answered with a smile. There were no warm lights in her eyes; only a dreamy, absent look.

'Good night. I adore you. Sleep well,' he said, and he kissed her hand and went away.

She stayed alone in a kind of reverie – a sort of stupor. Step by step she lived over every instant of the time she had been with Robert after he had entered Mademoiselle Reisz's door. She recalled his words, his looks. How few and meager they had been for her hungry heart! A vision – a transcendently seductive vision of a Mexican girl arose before her. She writhed with a jealous pang. She wondered when he would come back. He had not said he would come back. She had been with him, had heard his voice and touched his hand. But some way he had seemed nearer to her off there in Mexico.

XXXV

The morning was full of sunlight and hope. Edna could see before her no denial – only the promise of excessive joy. She lay in bed awake, with bright eyes full of speculation. 'He loves you, poor fool.' If she could but get that conviction firmly fixed in her mind, what mattered about the rest? She felt she had been childish and unwise the night before in giving herself over to despondency. She recapitulated the motives which no doubt explained Robert's reserve. They were not insurmountable; they would not hold if he really loved her; they could not hold against her own passion, which he must come to realize in time. She pictured him going to his business that morning. She even saw how he was dressed, how he walked down one street, and turned the corner of another, saw him bending over his desk, talking to people who entered the office, going to his lunch, and perhaps watching for her on the street. He would come to her in the afternoon or evening, sit and roll his cigarette, talk a little, and go away as he had done the night before. But how delicious it would be to have him there with her! She would have no regrets, nor seek to penetrate his reserve if he still chose to wear it.

Edna ate her breakfast only half dressed. The

maid brought her a delicious printed scrawl from Raoul, expressing his love, asking her to send him some bonbons, and telling her they had found that morning ten tiny white pigs all lying in a row beside Lidie's big white pig.

A letter also came from her husband, saying he hoped to be back early in March, and then they would get ready for that journey abroad which he had promised her so long, which he felt now fully able to afford; he felt able to travel as people should, without any thought of small economies – thanks to his recent speculations in Wall Street.

Much to her surprise she received a note from Arobin, written at midnight from the club. It was to say good morning to her, to hope that she had slept well, to assure her of his devotion, which he trusted she in some faintest manner returned.

All these letters were pleasing to her. She answered the children in a cheerful frame of mind, promising them bonbons, and congratulating them upon their happy find of the little pigs.

She answered her husband with friendly evasiveness, – not with any fixed design to mislead him, only because all sense of reality had gone out of her life; she had abandoned herself to Fate, and awaited the consequences with indifference.

To Arobin's note she made no reply. She put it under Celestine's stove lid.

Edna worked several hours with much spirit. She saw no one but a picture dealer, who asked her if it were true that she was going abroad to study in Paris.

She said possibly she might, and he negotiated with her for some Parisian studies to reach him in time for the holiday trade in December.

Robert did not come that day. She was keenly disappointed. He did not come the following day, nor the next. Each morning she awoke with hope, and each night she was a prey to despondency. She was tempted to seek him out. But far from yielding to the impulse, she avoided any occasion which might throw her in his way. She did not go to Mademoiselle Reisz's nor pass by Madame Lebrun's, as she might have done if he had still been in Mexico.

When Arobin, one night, urged her to drive with him, she went – out to the lake, on the Shell Road. His horses were full of mettle, and even a little unmanageable. She liked the rapid gait at which they spun along, and the quick, sharp sound of the horses' hoofs on the hard road. They did not stop anywhere to eat or to drink. Arobin was not needlessly imprudent. But they ate and they drank when they regained Edna's little dining room – which was comparatively early in the evening.

It was late when he left her. It was getting to be more than a passing whim with Arobin to see her and be with her. He had detected the latent sensuality, which unfolded under his delicate sense of her nature's requirements like a torpid, torrid, sensitive blossom.

There was no despondency when she fell asleep that night, nor was there hope when she awoke in the morning.

XXXVI

There was a garden out in the suburbs, a small, leafy corner, with a few green tables under the orange trees. An old cat slept all day on the stone step in the sun, and an old *mulatresse* slept her idle hours away in her chair at the open window, till someone happened to knock on one of the green tables. She had milk and cream cheese to sell, and bread and butter. There was no one who could make such excellent coffee or fry a chicken so golden brown as she.

The place was too modest to attract the attention of people of fashion, and so quiet as to have escaped the notice of those in search of pleasure and dissipation. Edna had discovered it accidentally one day when the high board gate stood ajar. She caught sight of a little green table, blotched with the checkered sunlight that filtered through the quivering leaves overhead. Within she had found the slumbering *mulatresse*, the drowsy cat, and a glass of milk which reminded her of the milk she had tasted in Iberville.

She often stopped there during her perambulations; sometimes taking a book with her, and sitting an hour or two under the trees when she found the place deserted. Once or twice she took a quiet dinner there alone, having instructed Celestine beforehand to prepare no dinner at home. It was the last place in the city where she would have expected to meet any one she knew.

Still she was not astonished when, as she was partaking of a modest dinner late in the afternoon, looking into an open book, stroking the cat, which had made friends with her – she was not greatly astonished to see Robert come in at the tall garden gate.

'I am destined to see you only by accident,' she said, shoving the cat off the chair beside her. He was surprised, ill at ease, almost embarrassed at meeting her thus so unexpectedly.

'Do you come here often?' he asked.

'I almost live here,' she said.

'I used to drop in very often for a cup of Catiche's good coffee. This is the first time since I came back.'

'She'll bring you a plate, and you will share my dinner. There's always enough for two – even three.' Edna had intended to be indifferent and as reserved as he when she met him; she had reached the determination by a laborious train of reasoning, incident to one of her despondent moods. But her resolve melted when she saw him before her, seated there beside her in the little garden, as if a designing Providence had led him into her path.

'Why have you kept away from me, Robert?' she asked, closing the book that lay open upon the table.

'Why are you so personal, Mrs Pontellier? Why

do you force me to idiotic subterfuges?' he exclaimed with sudden warmth. 'I suppose there's no use telling you I've been very busy, or that I've been sick, or that I've been to see you and not found you at home. Please let me off with any one of these excuses.'

'You are the embodiment of selfishness,' she said. 'You save yourself something – I don't know what – but there is some selfish motive, and in sparing yourself you never consider for a moment what I think, or how I feel your neglect and indifference. I suppose this is what you would call unwomanly; but I have got into a habit of expressing myself. It doesn't matter to me, and you may think me unwomanly if you like.'

'No; I only think you cruel, as I said the other day. Maybe not intentionally cruel; but you seem to be forcing me into disclosures which can result in nothing; as if you would have me bare a wound for the pleasure of looking at it, without the intention or power of healing it.'

'I'm spoiling your dinner, Robert; never mind what I say. You haven't eaten a morsel.'

'I only came in for a cup of coffee.' His sensitive face was all disfigured with excitement.

'Isn't this a delightful place?' she remarked. 'I am so glad it has never actually been discovered. It is so quiet, so sweet, here. Do you notice there is scarcely a sound to be heard? It's so out of the way; and a good walk from the car. However, I don't mind walking. I always feel so sorry for women who don't like to walk; they miss so much – so many rare little glimpses of life; and we women learn so little of life on the whole.

'Catiche's coffee is always hot. I don't know how she manages it, here in the open air. Celestine's coffee gets cold bringing it from the kitchen to the dining room. Three lumps! How can you drink it so sweet? Take some of the cress with your chop; it's so biting and crisp. Then there's the advantage of being able to smoke with your coffee out here. Now, in the city – aren't you going to smoke?'

'After a while,' he said, laying a cigar on the table.

'Who gave it to you?' she laughed.

'I bought it. I suppose I'm getting reckless; I bought a whole box.' She was determined not to be personal again and make him uncomfortable.

The cat made friends with him, and climbed into his lap when he smoked his cigar. He stroked her silky fur, and talked a little about her. He looked at Edna's book, which he had read; and he told her the end, to save her the trouble of wading through it, he said.

Again he accompanied her back to her home; and it was after dusk when they reached the little 'pigeon-house.' She did not ask him to remain, which he was grateful for, as it permitted him to stay without the discomfort of blundering through an excuse which he had no intention of considering. He helped her to light the lamp; then she went into her room to take off her hat and to bathe her face and hands.

When she came back Robert was not examining the pictures and magazines as before; he sat off in the shadow, leaning his head back on the chair as if in a reverie. Edna lingered a moment beside the table, arranging the books there. Then she went across the room to where he sat. She bent over the arm of his chair and called his name.

'Robert,' she said, 'are you asleep?'

'No,' he answered, looking up at her.

She leaned over and kissed him – a soft, cool, delicate kiss, whose voluptuous sting penetrated his whole being – then she moved away from him. He followed, and took her in his arms, just holding her close to him. She put her hand up to his face and pressed his cheek against her own. The action was full of love and tenderness. He sought her lips again. Then he drew her down upon the sofa beside him and held her hand in both of his.

'Now you know,' he said, 'now you know what I have been fighting against since last summer at Grand Isle, what drove me away and drove me back again.'

'Why have you been fighting against it?' she asked. Her face glowed with soft lights.

'Why? Because you were not free; you were Léonce Pontellier's wife. I couldn't help loving you if you were ten times his wife, but so long as I went away from you and kept away I could help telling you so.' She put her free hand up to his shoulder, and then against his cheek, rubbing it softly. He kissed her again. His face was warm and flushed.

'There in Mexico I was thinking of you all the time, and longing for you.'

'But not writing to me,' she interrupted.

'Something put into my head that you cared for me, and I lost my senses. I forgot everything but a wild dream of your some way becoming my wife.'

'Your wife!'

'Religion, loyalty, everything would give way if only you cared.'

'Then you must have forgotten that I was Léonce Pontellier's wife.'

'Oh! I was demented, dreaming of wild, impossible things, recalling men who had set their wives free, we have heard of such things.'

'Yes, we have heard of such things.'

'I came back full of vague, mad intentions. And when I got here – '

'When you got here you never came near me!' She was still caressing his cheek.

'I realized what a cur I was to dream of such a thing, even if you had been willing.'

She took his face between her hands and looked into it as if she would never withdraw her eyes more. She kissed him on the forehead, the eyes, the cheeks, and the lips.

'You have been a very, very foolish boy, wasting your time dreaming of impossible things when you speak of Mr Pontellier setting me free! I am no longer one of Mr Pontellier's possessions to dispose of or not. I give myself where I choose. If he were to say, "Here, Robert, take her and be happy, she is yours," I should laugh at you both.'

His face grew a little white. 'What do you mean?' he asked.

There was a knock at the door. Old Celestine came in to say that Madame Ratignolle's servant had come around the back way with a message that Madame had been taken sick and begged Mrs Pontellier to go to her immediately.

'Yes, yes,' said Edna, rising; 'I promised. Tell her yes – to wait for me. I'll go back with her.'

'Let me walk over with you,' offered Robert.

'No,' she said; 'I will go with the servant.' She went into her room to put on her hat, and when she came in again she sat once more upon the sofa beside him. He had not stirred. She put her arms about his neck.

'Good-by, my sweet Robert. Tell me good-by.' He kissed her with a degree of passion which had not before entered into his caress, and strained her to him.

'I love you,' she whispered, 'only you, no one but you. It was you who awoke me last summer out of a life-long, stupid dream. Oh! you have made me so unhappy with your indifference. Oh! I have suffered, suffered! Now you are here and we shall love each other, my Robert. We shall be everything to each other. Nothing else in the world is of any consequence. I must go to my friend; but you will wait for me? No matter how late; you will wait for me, Robert?'

'Don't go, don't go! Oh! Edna, stay with me,' he pleaded. 'Why should you go? Stay with me, stay with me.'

'I shall come back as soon as I can; I shall find you here.' She buried her face in his neck, and said good-by again. Her seductive voice, together with his great love for her, had enthralled his senses, had deprived him of every impulse but the longing to hold her and keep her.

XXXVII

Edna looked in at the drug store. Monsieur Ratignolle was putting up a mixture himself, very carefully, dropping a red liquid into a tiny glass. He was grateful to Edna for having come, her presence would be a comfort to his wife. Madame Ratignolle's sister, who had always been with her at such trying times, had not been able to come up from the plantation, and Adèle had been inconsolable until Mrs Pontellier so kindly promised to come to her. The nurse had been with them at night for the past week, as she lived a great distance away. And Doctor Mandelet had been coming and going all the afternoon. They were then looking for him any moment.

Edna hastened upstairs by a private stairway that led from the rear of the store to the apartments above. The children were all sleeping in a back room. Madame Ratignolle was in the salon, whither she had strayed in her suffering impatience. She sat on the sofa, clad in an ample white *peignoir*, holding a handkerchief tight in her hand with a nervous clutch. Her face was drawn and pinched, her sweet blue eyes haggard and unnatural. All her beautiful hair had been drawn back and plaited. It lay in a long braid on the sofa pillow, coiled like a golden serpent. The nurse, a comfortable looking *Griffe* woman in white apron and cap, was urging her to return to her bedroom.

'There is no use, there is no use,' she said at once to Edna. 'We must get rid of Mandelet; he is getting too old and careless. He said he would be here at half-past seven; now it must be eight. See what time it is, Josephine.'

The woman was possessed of a cheerful nature, and refused to take any situation too seriously, especially a situation with which she was so familar. She urged Madame to have courage and patience. But Madame only set her teeth hard into her under lip, and Edna saw the sweat gather in beads on her white forehead. After a moment or two she uttered a profound sigh and wiped her face with the handkerchief rolled in a ball. She appeared exhausted. The nurse gave her a fresh handkerchief, sprinkled with cologne water.

'This is too much!' she cried. 'Mandelet ought to be killed! Where is Alphonse? Is it possible I am to be abandoned like this – neglected by everyone?'

'Neglected, indeed!' exclaimed the nurse. Wasn't she there? And here was Mrs Pontellier leaving, no doubt, a pleasant evening at home to devote to her? And wasn't Monsieur Ratignolle coming that very instant through the hall? And Josephine was quite sure she had heard Doctor Mandelet's coupé. Yes, there it was, down at the door.

Adèle consented to go back to her room. She sat on the edge of a little low couch next to her bed.

Doctor Mandelet paid no attention to Madame

Ratignolle's upbraidings. He was accustomed to them at such times, and was too well convinced of her loyalty to doubt it.

He was glad to see Edna, and wanted her to go with him into the salon and entertain him. But Madame Ratignolle would not consent that Edna should leave her for an instant. Between agonizing moments, she chatted a little, and said it took her mind off her sufferings.

Edna began to feel uneasy. She was seized with a vague dread. Her own like experiences seemed far away, unreal, and only half remembered. She recalled faintly an ectasy of pain, the heavy odor of chloroform, a stupor which had deadened sensation, and an awakening to find a little new life to which she had given being, added to the great unnumbered multitude of souls that come and go.

She began to wish she had not come; her presence was not necessary. She might have invented a pretext for staying away; she might even invent a pretext now for going. But Edna did not go. With an inward agony, with a flaming, outspoken revolt against the ways of Nature, she witnessed the scene of torture.

She was still stunned and speechless with emotion when later she leaned over her friend to kiss her and softly say good-by. Adèle, pressing her cheek, whispered in an exhausted voice: 'Think of the children, Edna. Oh think of the children! Remember them!'

XXXVIII

Edna still felt dazed when she got outside in the open air. The Doctor's coupé had returned for him and stood before the *porte cochère*. She did not wish to enter the coupé, and told Doctor Mandelet she would walk; she was not afraid, and would go alone. He directed his carriage to meet him at Mrs Pontellier's, and he started to walk home with her.

Up – away up, over the narrow street between the tall houses, the stars were blazing. The air was mild and caressing, but cool with the breath of spring and the night. They walked slowly, the Doctor with a heavy, measured tread and his hands behind him; Edna, in an absent-minded way, as she had walked one night at Grand Isle, as if her thoughts had gone ahead of her and she was striving to overtake them.

'You shouldn't have been there, Mrs Pontellier,' he said. 'That was no place for you. Adèle is full of whims at such times. There were a dozen women she might have had with her, unimpressionable women. I felt that it was cruel, cruel. You shouldn't have gone.'

'Oh, well!' she answered, indifferently. 'I don't know that it matters after all. One has to think of the children some time or other, the sooner the better.'

'When is Léonce coming back?'

'Quite soon. Some time in March.'

'And you are going abroad?'

'Perhaps – no, I am not going. I'm not going to be forced into doing things. I don't want to go abroad. I want to be let alone. Nobody has any right – except children, perhaps – and even then, it seems to me – or it did seem – ' She felt that her speech was voicing the incoherency of her thoughts, and stopped abruptly.

'The trouble is,' sighed the Doctor, grasping her meaning intuitively, 'that youth is given up to illusions. It seems to be a provision of Nature, a decoy to secure mothers for the race. And Nature takes no account of moral consequences, or arbitrary conditions which we create, and which we feel obliged to maintain at any cost.'

'Yes,' she said. 'The years that are gone seem like dreams – if one might go on sleeping and dreaming – but to wake up and find – oh! well! perhaps it is better to wake up after all, even to suffer, rather than to remain a dupe to illusions all one's life.'

'It seems to me, my dear child,' said the Doctor at parting, holding her hand, 'you seem to me to be in trouble. I am not going to ask for your confidence. I will only say that if ever you feel moved to give it to me, perhaps I might help you. I know I would understand, and I tell you there are not many who would – not many, my dear.'

'Some way I don't feel moved to speak of things that trouble me. Don't think I am ungrateful or that I don't appreciate your sympathy. There are periods of despondency and suffering which take possession of me. But I don't want anything but my own way. That is wanting a good deal, of course, when you have to trample upon the lives, the hearts, the prejudices of others – but no matter – still, I shouldn't want to trample upon the little lives. Oh! I don't know what I'm saying, Doctor. Good night. Don't blame me for anything.'

'Yes, I will blame you if you don't come and see me soon. We will talk of things you never have dreamt of talking about before. It will do us both good. I don't want you to blame yourself, whatever comes. Good night, my child.'

She let herself in at the gate, but instead of entering she sat upon the step of the porch. The night was quiet and soothing. All the tearing emotion of the last few hours seemed to fall away from her like a somber, uncomfortable garment, which she had but to loosen to be rid of. She went back to that hour before Adèle had sent for her; and her senses kindled afresh in thinking of Robert's words, the pressure of his arms, and the feeling of his lips upon her own. She could picture at that moment no greater bliss on earth than possession of the beloved one. His expression of love had already given him to her in part. When she thought that he was there at hand, waiting for her, she grew numb with the intoxication of expectancy. It was so late;

he would be asleep perhaps. She would awaken him with a kiss. She hoped he would be asleep that she might arouse him with her caresses.

Still she remembered Adèle's voice whispering, 'Think of the children; think of them.' She meant to think of them; that determination had driven into her soul like a death wound – but not tonight. Tomorrow would be time to think of everything.

Robert was not waiting for her in the little parlor. He was nowhere at hand. The house was empty. But he had scrawled on a piece of paper that lay in the lamp-light:

'I love you. Good-by – because I love you.'

Edna grew faint when she read the words. She went and sat on the sofa. Then she stretched herself out there, never uttering a sound. She did not sleep. She did not go to bed. The lamp sputtered and went out. She was still awake in the morning, when Celestine unlocked the kitchen door and came in to light the fire.

XXXIX

Victor, with hammer and nails and scraps of scantling, was patching a corner of one of the galleries. Mariequita sat near by, dangling her legs, watching him work, and handing him nails from the tool box. The sun was beating down upon them. The girl had covered her head with her apron folded into a square pad. They had been talking for an hour or more. She was never tired of hearing Victor describe the dinner at Mrs Pontellier's. He exaggerated every detail, making it appear a veritable Lucillean feast. The flowers were in tubs, he said. The champagne was quaffed from huge golden goblets. Venus rising from the foam could have presented no more entrancing a spectacle than Mrs Pontellier, blazing with beauty and diamonds at the head of the board, while the other women were all of them youthful houris, possessed of incomparable charms.

She got it into her head that Victor was in love with Mrs Pontellier, and he gave her evasive answers, framed so as to confirm her belief. She grew sullen and cried a little, threatening to go off and leave him to his fine ladies. There were a dozen men crazy about her at the *Chênière*, and since it was the fashion to be in love with married people, why, she could run away any time she liked to New Orleans with Célina's husband.

Célina's husband was a fool, a coward, and a pig, and to prove it to her, Victor intended to hammer his head into a jelly the next time he encountered him. This assurance was very consoling to Mariequita. She dried her eyes, and grew cheerful at the prospect.

They were still talking of the dinner and the allurements of city life when Mrs Pontellier herself slipped around the corner of the house. The two youngsters stayed dumb with amazement before what they considered to be an apparition. But it was really she in flesh and blood, looking tired and a little travel-stained.

'I walked up from the wharf,' she said, 'and heard the hammering. I supposed it was you, mending the porch. It's a good thing. I was always tripping over those loose planks last summer. How dreary and deserted everything looks!'

It took Victor some little time to comprehend that she had come in Beaudelet's lugger, that she had come alone, and for no purpose but to rest.

'There's nothing fixed up yet, you see. I'll give you my room; it's the only place.'

'Any corner will do,' she assured him.

'And if you can stand Philomel's cooking,' he went on, 'though I might try to get her mother while you are here. Do you think she would come?' turning to Mariequita.

Mariequita thought that perhaps Philomel's

mother might come for a few days, and money enough.

Beholding Mrs Pontellier make her appearance, the girl had at once suspected a lovers' rendezvous. But Victor's astonishment was so genuine, and Mrs Pontellier's indifference so apparent, that the disturbing notion did not lodge long in her brain. She contemplated with the greatest interest this woman who gave the most sumptuous dinners in America, and who had all the men in New Orleans at her feet.

'What time will you have dinner?' asked Edna. 'I'm very hungry; but don't get anything extra.'

'I'll have it ready in little or no time,' he said, bustling and packing away his tools. 'You may go to my room to brush up and rest yourself. Mariequita will show you.'

'Thank you,' said Edna. 'But, do you know, I have a notion to go down to the beach and take a good wash and even a little swim, before dinner?'

'The water is too cold!' they both exclaimed. 'Don't think of it.'

'Well, I might go down and try – dip my toes in. Why, it seems to me the sun is hot enough to have warmed the very depths of the ocean. Could you get me a couple of towels? I'd better go right away, so as to be back in time. It would be a little too chilly if I waited till this afternoon.'

Mariequita ran over to Victor's room and returned with some towels, which she gave to Edna.

'I hope you have fish for dinner,' said Edna, as

she started to walk away, 'but don't do anything extra if you haven't.'

'Run and find Philomel's mother,' Victor instructed the girl. 'I'll go to the kitchen and see what I can do. By Gimminy! Women have no consideration! She might have sent me word.'

Edna walked on down to the beach rather mechanically, not noticing anything special except that the sun was hot. She was not dwelling upon any particular train of thought. She had done all the thinking which was necessary after Robert went away, when she lay awake upon the sofa till morning.

She had said over and over to herself: 'Today it is Arobin; tomorrow it will be someone else. It makes no difference to me, it doesn't matter about Léonce Pontellier – but Raoul and Étienne!' She understood now clearly what she had meant long ago when she said to Adèle Ratignolle that she would give up the unessential, but she would never sacrifice herself for her children.

Despondency had come upon her there in the wakeful night, and had never lifted. There was no one thing in the world that she desired. There was no human being whom she wanted near her except Robert; and she even realized that the day would come when he, too, and the thought of him would melt out of her existence, leaving her alone. The children appeared before her like antagonists who had overcome her, who had overpowered and sought to drag her into the soul's slavery for the rest of her days. But she knew a way to elude them. She was not thinking of these things when she walked down to the beach.

The water of the Gulf stretched out before her, gleaming with the million lights of the sun. The voice of the sea is seductive, never ceasing, whispering, clamoring, murmuring, inviting the soul to wander in abysses of solitude. All along the white beach, up and down, there was no living thing in sight. A bird with a broken wing was beating the air above, reeling, fluttering, circling disabled down, down to the water.

Edna had found her old bathing suit still hanging, faded, upon its accustomed peg.

She put it on, leaving her clothing in the bathhouse. But when she was there beside the sea, absolutely alone, she cast the unpleasant, pricking garments from her, and for the first time in her life she stood naked in the open air, at the mercy of the sun, the breeze that beat upon her, and the waves that invited her.

How strange and awful it seemed to stand naked under the sky! how delicious! She felt like some new-born creature, opening its eyes in a familiar world that it had never known.

The foamy wavelets curled up to her white feet, and coiled like serpents about her ankles. She walked out. The water was chill, but she walked on. The water was deep, but she lifted her white body and reached out with a long, sweeping stroke. The touch of the sea is sensuous, enfolding the body in its soft, close embrace.

She went on and on. She remembered the night she swam far out, and recalled the terror that seized her at the fear of being unable to regain the shore. She did not look back now, but went on and on, thinking of the bluegrass meadow that she had traversed when a little child, believing that it had no beginning and no end.

Her arms and legs were growing tired.

She thought of Léonce and the children. They were a part of her life. But they need not have thought that they could possess her, body and soul. How Mademoiselle Reisz would have laughed, perhaps sneered, if she knew! 'And you call yourself an artist! What pretensions, Madame! The artist must possess the courageous soul that dares and defies.'

Exhaustion was pressing upon and overpowering her.

'Good-by – because I love you.' He did not know; he did not understand. He would never understand. Perhaps Doctor Mandelet would have understood if she had seen him – but it was too late; the shore was far behind her, and her strength was gone.

She looked into the distance, and the old terror flamed up for an instant, then sank again. Edna heard her father's voice and her sister Margaret's. She heard the barking of an old dog that was chained to the sycamore tree. The spurs of the cavalry officer clanged as he walked across the porch. There was the hum of bees, and the musky odor of pinks filled the air.

TITLES IN EVERYMAN'S LIBRARY

This book is set in EHRHARDT. The precise origin
of the typeface is unclear. Most of the founts were
probably cut by the Hungarian punch-cutter
Nicholas Kis for the Ehrhardt foundry
in Leipzig, where they were left
for sale in 1689. In 1938 the
Monotype foundry pro-
duced the modern
version.